ADAM MONK

Rise by the Sun Dance by the Moon

Copyright © 2020 by Adam Monk

All rights reserved. No part of this publication may be reproduced, stored or transmitted in any form or by any means, electronic, mechanical, photocopying, recording, scanning, or otherwise without written permission from the publisher. It is illegal to copy this book, post it to a website, or distribute it by any other means without permission.

First edition

This book was professionally typeset on Reedsy. Find out more at reedsy.com

Acknowledgement

Julie Hoyle for editing the book

Bailey McGinn for Designing the cover

Chapter 1

The rain creates streams in the street, gushing into the drains and in the dark, it resembles thick oil. A young man emerges from an alleyway and walks through the stream, cutting the flow as he crosses the street to the riverbank. He stares, focused on a single spot where the guttering is leaking on a café next to the bridge. Drip ... drip ... drip. Now he focuses on the bridge and slowly walks towards it, one hand now on the railing of the bridge, softly gliding along. All his senses are heightened; he can hear the rain colliding with the river, the water gushing into the drains, the smell of wet metal and he feels a hair-raising chill on his skin. He dumps his jacket on the floor. The young man climbs over the railing of the bridge and stares into the river that is being attacked by the rain above. He can almost hear each individual rain droplet whistling through the air before hitting the water. Drip ... drip ... drip. Hands are now off the railing. A shallow breath creates a cold cloud of air that disperses into the night. Eyes close, a tear rolling down his cheek combining with the rain already running down his face. Body begins to let go – he falls.

An old man in his beaten-up, paint-peeled boat saw the young man on the bridge. He too could almost hear the individual rain droplets, but these were crackling on the wooden roof of his boat and dribbling down like little waterfalls over the windows. The old man moved close to the window and the warmth from his breath made condensation which blocked his view of the bridge. Through the window, he could only see a silhouette of the young man. He moved out onto the deck and immediately, the rain soaked through to his bones and started running down the cracks in his sun-kissed face. His eyes, crystal green, gazed upon the young man and before the rain droplets had ran off his face, the young man fell.

"No!" he cried out. Without hesitation the old man ran and jumped into the river. On such a cold winter's night, the icy water took his breath away. Once he composed himself, he began to swim towards the young man. The clothes he wore began to weigh him down; he began to feel heavy and his bones were cold now.

As he reached him, the young man lay face down and lifeless in the water. The old man shook him and he muttered to himself, with desperation, "You're a fighter. There's fight in you left. Don't quit on me." He got no response so swam with the young man draped over his hip until he reached the riverbank; once there, he pulled him ashore. A few moments of chilling uncertainty passed: nothing, not a breath or flicker of life. The old man was sure he was gone; he was pale like a ghost, lips turned blue, and death filled the air. He sat with the young man's head on his lap and all he could think was why, why did he do it?

Then, the young man violently coughed, his chest sharply contracting. Water began to trickle out of the side of his mouth and ran down his face. He gasped for air and began frantically panting. The first thing he saw was the old man's crystal-green eyes staring at him, and the first thing he felt was the old man

CHAPTER 1

holding him and the rain coming down on them both.

The old man carried the young man back to the boat. For the young man, all was blurred; the cold had numbed and distorted his senses. The old man told him to focus on a London street sign that read: London Borough of Greenwich. A streetlight above lit up the sign with a warm orange glow. For a second, the old man's attention moved to the raindrops in front of the sign and the orange glow of the streetlight gave the chilling droplets life. Then, once the old man had got them both to his boat, he helped the young man into the cabin, pushing open the door with his one free arm. He sat him down then closed the door that was now swinging in the wind. The young man could still hear the dripping; this time it came from the young man himself. Drip, drip, drip. Water droplets hit the floor as they ran off his hand.

"I'm Richard, by the way," the old man said and ran his fingers through his long thick wavy grey hair. He got them both blankets then started making some tea. The young man sat there shivering, despite the heavy wool blanket laid over his shoulders. He was crouched over trying to warm himself up, rubbing his arms in the hope of finding warmth.

With a shivering stutter in his voice, the young man said, "My name's ..." He couldn't get any more words out; he was too cold. The old man told him to rest. They would talk tomorrow, he said.

Once the kettle had boiled, the old man made them both some tea then sat down opposite the young man and said nothing. He knew now was not the time to talk. So, they sat there with the sound of rain beating down on the wooden roof, drinking their tea.

The young man went to the bathroom once he had stopped

shivering and found some warmth. He stood there, leaning over the sink, staring at himself in the mirror. Puddles of water built up in his eyes and tears rolled down his face. He must have looked at himself for an hour, not breaking eye contact with himself once. He cried at the thought of tomorrow and tomorrow's tomorrow.

The old man sat outside the door wrapped up in his blanket, listening and guarding the young man from his mind. The tears of this young man shattered the old man's heart. How could someone so young be in so much pain? he thought to himself. He was a casualty of a flawed system. The old man hadn't heard anything for a while, so he turned and faced the door.

"You OK?" he said through a little crack between the door and the frame. The young man had dropped to his knees; he couldn't stand to look at himself any longer. After hearing the old man, he stood up and looked at himself in the mirror one last time, and aggressively rubbed his hands over his face, screaming inside. He looked into his own eyes and saw nothing but sadness and sorrow. One last tear fell from his face before he eventually came out of the bathroom and fell asleep on the old man's shoulder.

The old man couldn't sleep that night, but dawn was just round the corner. The sun rose early the next morning; clear skies with the orange rays warming the cabin and making the river glimmer and shine. The young man woke up alone on the sofa in the cabin, with the morning light beaming through the gaps in the curtains and under the crack in the door. The old man had placed a pillow under his head . This small act comforted the young man and brought a smile to his face. He then went outside onto the deck where the old man was having his morning coffee in his three-legged chair. This chair had

CHAPTER 1

travelled all around the world with him, from tropical islands of the Pacific, to the Mediterranean, to the coasts of the Americas, even to the Indian Ocean and Asia. The old man had set up a chair next to him ready for the young man; this chair had four legs. They both sat there looking at the clear morning sky, not a cloud in sight. The young man cleared his throat and said, "Thank you." The old man looked at him, gave him a father-like nod, then turned back and continued looking at the morning sky

A couple of minutes of silence passed and then, after building up the words in his mind, the young man took a deep breath and said, "I feel out of control. I feel like a feather in the wind, aimlessly drifting. I feel powerless, like my life has been put on a predetermined course; imagine getting into a taxi where the driver knows where you're going but you don't. My life is the taxi ride and I am merely a witness to the journey. I have no clue who I am or how I can find out who I am, and I feel empty, just empty and so lost. Society's version of success doesn't compute with me; its rules and expectations corrode my soul. This world is so big, with so much possibility, and trying to find my place in it is driving me insane. I crave meaning, a reason for being. I want something to feel passionate about, but I have no clue what, and the pressure life and society puts on you to know now, is unbearable. That's why I let go of the railings on the bridge. I had lost hope in finding meaning. I had lost the little glimmer of hope I held so dearly. I tried for so long to keep going, I really did. I read books, watched videos, even had a little bit of counselling. But none of that could change the fact I'm lost and hurting. If people could see my mental wounds, they wouldn't tell me to man up, get on with it, stop feeling sorry for myself. It took every ounce of energy I had but I just got so tired. I stared at the revolver in my mind; I would stare for hours, begging for the trigger to be pulled."

A few tears ran down the young man's face, rolling off his cheeks and onto his hands, then splashed onto the deck.

The old man's eyes had a look of sadness and familiarity to the young man's words. A few moments passed and the old man thought to himself, this may be the last thing I do, but I will restore hope and meaning to this young man's life or at least guide him onto the path. I may not be able to help a dying generation, but I can help one of its members.

He then asked, "Would you like to spend some time with me? I can teach you to sail."

The young man looked upon the river which was still glittering from the rising sun and said, "Yes."

A little smile appeared on the young man's face – the old man's eyes now showed a sense of hope. They both leaned back in their chairs, no words, not a sound, but no words were like a thousand words and those silent thousand words were a blanket of hope for the young man. They drank their bitter black coffee with swirls of steam rising from the mugs dispersing into the mist of the morning air. The old man had one condition for the young man staying with him; he had to write everyday in a diary. He said it could be a sentence or a novel as long as it was true and from the heart. The young man happily agreed although he thought it was an odd condition to have. He was expecting a long list of rules but no, all he had to do was write.

Later that day the old man took the young man on his first sailing lesson. He thought he would take him out on the water straight away so the young man couldn't change his mind, so up the river they went which gradually widened until they reached the sea. Little did they expect it but they rather enjoyed each other's company – the old man was becoming like the father the young man had never had. His first lesson went well; the old man had taught the young man in the same way an old friend had taught him many years ago. He picked up everything he was taught, and quickly too; the old man liked that as he didn't like repeating himself.

One thing the young man noticed was how tough and worn the man's hands were as years of handling ropes and rigging had left them scarred and leathery. But that wasn't the most noticeable part of the old man's hands. He had two swallows tattooed on them, one on each, on the back of his hands between the index finger and thumb. The ink had faded and the lines blurred a little. The young man was surprised he hadn't noticed them sooner then asked if there was a meaning to his tattoos.

The old man explained, "I met a sailor who was in the Royal Navy while in Portsmouth, years ago now, and the sailor had these swallows tattooed on his hands. We got talking and he told me that they were signs of an experienced sailor. By then I had sailed thousands of miles, so I had the experience. But the reason I got the tattoos, and I got them the same day that I met the sailor, was that he told me the swallows would carry me to heaven if I ever drowned. He said it was a tradition that started in the navy and went back years. Now, I'm not much of a religious man but I liked them as good luck charms. And now, over the years, my good luck charms have been weathered by the sea." The young man smiled. That would be the first of hundreds of stories to come. The old man added, "I didn't tell Ruby I was getting them done and she wasn't a fan of the tattoos at first but after a week, she admitted she rather liked them."

As they made their way ashore, the old man told stories of his travels and his great love, Ruby. His eyes lit up when he spoke about her. After they had met, they went travelling the world together and lived a fairy tale love very few get to have. But it wasn't a fairy tale love like you see in the movies; they had a fairy tale love that they fought for, argued for and most of all had to commit to. Pictures of their adventures and love were stuck to the walls of the boat's cabin.

The young man said, "She was beautiful."

Richard's reply was, "She still is." His late wife was very much alive in his heart, so her beauty remained very much alive. The young man looked at the pictures on the cabin wall, in awe of his adventures and in awe of his love with Ruby; by the look of the pictures, the old man had really lived.

After hearing the old man's stories of his travels, the young man had begun to dream things he never could have possibly imagined before – dreams of travelling the world with freedom running through his hair, unknown adventures and possibilities on the horizon. He never though people like him could travel; he thought he was destined to live the life society wanted for him. He thought travel was reserved for the wealthy, but the old man's husky words installed hope into the young man's heart and mind that he too could live a life like his.

The young man asked, "May I ask how you afforded your travels?"

, "Well, on my first trips, my friends and I worked at every place we went to and shared everything. My later trips were funded by investments I had made, some inheritance and with work I did that was well paid. I was quite lucky. I could be anywhere in the world for work and I met the right people at the right time," the old man answered.

The young man said, "This may ... no, this is going to sound stupid, but I'm glad I jumped off that bridge."

"Why on earth are you glad you did that?"

The young man's reply brought a tear to the old man's eye, which, like the rain, ran through the cracks in his cheek and was then lost into wilderness of what was the old man's scruffy beard.

"It helped me find you and I'm so glad I did."

The old man would set the alarm early; the sun would still be sleeping when he rose. He made the young man get up with him, which at first was a struggle; he was undisciplined, which would quickly change. During the first week, the old man practically had to kick him out of bed or entice him with freshy made coffee which he would place on a chair just far enough away that he had to get out of bed to get it. In the first week the old man would always say, "You can sleep when your dead. You owe it to the day to be awake and living. On Sundays you can sleep in; Sunday is for rest."

One morning in the first few days they spent together, the young man wrote a diary entry. "I miss the nights I never went out into, I miss the friends I never hung out with, I miss the rules I never broke, I miss the young love I never had, I miss the mistakes I never made, I miss the rebellion I never took part in, I miss the memories I never made. I don't miss the fear, the anxiety, and the pain, no I don't miss that at all."

A few weeks went by. The young man and the old man had spent every day together and were now awfully close, so close, in fact, it was like they had known each other their entire lives. The young man had begun to write in his diary with a yearning and a desire for life, which warmed the old man's heart. He knew the young man still had pain in his heart; his mind was still a maze and that his demons would come out to play just to remind him they were there. But the young man was beginning to win some battles and he was day by day getting a little better, taking tiny steps forward. The old man would remind the young man that mental health may seem like one battle, but it's not. It's a war that may never end, but you will start to win more and more battles and your courage to continue fighting is what matters. The enemy will grow tired.

The young man's most recent writing read, "I would die for passion. I would fall on the sword of love a thousand times if it meant a life of passion. Feed my soul for it is hungry. Feed my soul for it needs passion. Feed my soul or it will die..

The young man was not bad at sailing now either but still had lots of lessons to learn. The old man knew he was a natural, he was a man of the sea. He told the young man he must have the blood of Poseidon in his veins – he would now sail alone under the watchful eye of the old man who was always at the ready to make a cheeky sarcastic remark. The old man had given the young man purpose, a new-found desire for life and, dare I say, had become a dear friend. The young man had been living on the boat with the old man since the night of the bridge and heavy god-like rain.

The pair had now begun to fix up the boat, getting her ready for a long journey. They planned to do it little by little so they could still sail as much as possible; they didn't want her bound to land while fixing her. One afternoon they sat on the deck of the boat and planned the mini restoration.

The old man would read the young man's diary entries while he was out doing the food shopping or getting the supplies they needed for the boat. He wanted to make sure he was fulfilling the one condition he had made, but also he wanted to check the young man was OK because sometimes the written word can say what the spoken cannot. The young man caught the old man reading the diary once and the old man jumped up, about to plead for forgiveness, but before he could do that, the young man said, "Don't worry, I leave it out so you can read it. I don't want you thinking I'm breaking your one rule." The old man smiled and chuckled as he closed the diary.

The young man would ask quite frequently in a number of ways, "Why spend money restoring the boat? She is perfectly suitable for our sailing." The old man would never answer when the young man asked that question; the only response would be a little nod, but never any words. By now the pair had spent a lot of time together and as they were having dinner – the old man's famous (how famous we will never know exactly, but for argument's sake, let's just say it was world renowned) vegetable pie – they dug in and the old man said, "Hey ... should anything happen to me, I want you to have my boat and travel the world. Make memories as I did, live a life without regret as I did and maybe, if you're lucky, meet a woman and fall in love. Oh, I miss my Ruby ... I consider you a son." The young man smiled while looking down at his food.

The old man looked at the young man and said, "Look at me for a moment. I want you to live, really live, take risks, and live courageously! Life is so short, my friend, so, so short. So live hard, love passionately and live a life of your choosing." There's not enough time for me to teach you all I have learned. You're just going to have to let life be your mentor – life has a pretty good way of teaching us if we are willing to be its pupils. All the greatest teachers in the world are really just great pupils."

"You're not dying, are you?" the young man asked.

"We all will one day," the old man replied. "Just promise me you will travel and live the life of your choosing, promise me."

"I promise" the young man replied. The old man then gave his nod, scratched his beard and ran his fingers through his hair before digging into more vegetable pie.

With each passing day the boat became more and more seaworthy. She could handle coastal sailing, but she needed a little fixing and love to be worthy of a long voyage – it was hard work fixing a boat when you only had two people, but they enjoyed it. It was toughening up the young man's hands. They enjoyed spending all day together; they would talk for hours telling stories and then sometimes spend hours in silence. But no matter what they did, they just liked spending time together. Fixing the boat and learning to sail grounded the young man while he tried to figure out his mind. The young man and the old man talked through every thought he'd had. For many nights at the beginning they would talk well into the early hours of the morning when he couldn't sleep or when the young man would wake up in a pool of sweat. The old man would put the kettle on and they would talk, or not. Sometimes the old man would just sit there with him. Just having him there when his demons came out to play made things a lot better. With each conversation they had, the young man felt his mind ease a little and become a little clearer.

The young man had fallen in love with the ocean and sailing. So far the old man had helped him sail the boat in one way or another, but as they made their way up the river that was gradually widening, the old man said, "Think you can sail her alone?"

The young man replied, "I don't know, you think so?"

"Thee have little faith. I suppose we will find out, won't we?" the old man said. He sat back enjoying the sea breeze blowing

CHAPTER 1

on his face, savouring the moment, while the young man fended for himself on the open waters. He had sailed alone before but this time he wouldn't have the watchful eye of the old man. The old man's only words to him were, "Breath and enjoy."

The young man glided over the waves and everything seamlessly came together. While the young man sailed, the old man just sat in awe of the man he had become and the man he would become. He sat there thinking how proud he was.

Little did the young man know but he was slowly becoming the old man. He had grown his hair long and had a little stubble now too, which he hoped would become a beard one day. The young man was quite handsome and when young women walked by the boat, they would stare with desire in their eyes and give blushing smiles with little waves. The old man loved teasing the young man about all the attention he got. The old man would laugh hard at his own jokes, while the young man smiled, shaking his head in disapproval of the jokes. The old man would whistle at the young man to get his attention and when he looked, the old man would brush his hair to the side with a flick and wave at the young man liked the ladies did. He couldn't hold a straight face for long and would burst out laughing. this, the young man would laugh at. Humour was a big part of their relationship; no time of day, no situation was ever a bad time to tease or joke.

Their daily routine consisted of morning coffee and a sunrise on the deck, fixing the boat, sailing the boat, and sharing stories and jokes over a beer after a long day. Simple but that's how they liked it; the old man would always say "simplicity is underrated!"

By now three months had passed. The old man became more fragile as the days went on and he started to develop a chesty cough that rattled the windows in the cabin. This worried the young man; he would beg the old man to see a doctor, but he would always say he was fine and would also say there was nothing they could do for him. For a second, the young man began to imagine living life without his newly found friend, father figure and mentor. This saddened the young man and tears began to fall from his eyes. The old man appeared. The young man wiped his face and sniffled, rubbing his nose on the chunky roll neck the old man had given him which was a tad too big. They spent the evening just like any other evening with a cold beer. With the radio gently playing in the background, they watched intently as the sun set. They both looked up at the night sky and a little later the young man got up to go to bed. He said goodnight to the old man, and before he got into the cabin the old man said to him, "I'm proud of you." The young man gave a nod and then the old man said good night. He looked up at the night sky and smiled, not just a smile, a real smile, a beaming smile. Then he fell asleep under the moonlit sky.

As dawn broke the young man woke up, eyes half open, but something was off. The fresh smell of coffee, which normally accompanied the morning sun, wasn't there. As the young man walked out onto the deck, he saw the old man still lying in his three-legged chair. The morning sun shone brightly and bounced off the greys of the old man's hair and the young man knew he was at peace with his Ruby. Tears began to fall down his face. He walked over, took the old man's hand and just held it. He knew he was gone but a part of him was still hoping he would feel a squeeze and he would have the old man back.

Chapter 2

It was the next morning – no coffee, no old man. All the young man had was the morning sun and a letter from the old man, with some simple words that would be with him forever.

"To my young friend, my son. Please don't be mad but I knew my days were numbered I wanted our time together to be joyful and full of hope. The more I think about it, I think we were destined to meet; My Ruby would have loved you and we will be watching over you. My last words to you, my son. The courageous may lose but the wary never win. Remember, life is short and precious. So live hard, love passionately, forgive quickly, and follow your heart – live the life of your creation and make that creation a true reflection of yourself. Also make sure to love yourself, respect yourself and be kind to yourself; nobody will if you don't. Look after that beautiful mind of yours.

Sometimes in life we find ourselves in situations where we can't control what's happening, but there's one thing we can control;, the way we respond to what's happening.

Also, please don't try and find happiness. It is not something you can find. There is no destination for happiness. Happiness is a choice and our actions dictate that You must choose to be happy every day, whether that happiness comes from a cup of coffee or a conversation or even the wind, happiness is a choice. Please choose it – love and happiness is the real essence of life.

The stuff that scares you to death is probably the stuff worth doing. One foot in the comfort zone and one foot out of the comfort zone is how I liked to live; you never know, that might work for you.

Don't feel like you have to follow society's rules of how to live life, I didn't and had a great time. The system is designed for the system to thrive. It doesn't take people into account. People aren't systems, they are souls and souls need to be fed passion, you yourself said that.

Don't listen to people who think your way of life is wrong. Try as they may to fill your head with doubt and fear, but nobody knows you, how you know yourself, so don't let the fear and doubt in. Don't become a predictable robot. It's safe to say their advice is not needed as they have not the courage to walk their own path and so criticise yours. At the end of the day, if you can look back on your life and say I lived, truly lived in whatever way that means for you, then you will have succeeded in a way not many get to.

One of my favourite quotes is from Sir Winston Churchill. He said, 'Success is not final, failure is not fatal: it is the courage to continue that counts.' And you, my son, are the most courageous man I have ever met and I'm proud of the man you have become. As I write this letter, I find myself trying to give you a lifetime's worth of lessons. Just remember, life is short and precious so LIVE. LIVE. LIVE!

Ps. I've left you the boat and all my money. Now don't be sad, I haven't left as I'm in your heart and you can always find me in sunrises, sunsets and the stars of the night. Get on with this adventure called life!

Love, Richard x

The young man gently folded the letter and put it back in the now crinkled envelope. The old man had drawn Poseidon's spear at the bottom of the page. He smiled at this and took it as a symbol of the voyage he was going to undertake.

After a few moments of distant gazing and pondering, the young man went for a walk. He must have walked for miles. Sweat lined the rim of his face and slowly tricked down. He came across a café called Isabelle's next to a common and sat at a table outside. A young lady came wearing a denim apron with Isabelle's sewn on in pink.

"Hi," she said. "I'm Ruby. I'll be your waitress. Can I get you anything?"

The young man smiled and thought of the old man. "Ruby's a lovely a name," he said, then just ordered a tea. Where he sat, the sun was blocked by a tree, a huge oak tree. The shade was nice as it was a scorching hot day. After she had brought the tea, the young man asked the waitress for a pen. Using napkins from the table to write on, he began to plan his travels. He had studied maps with the old man so he could draw them off by heart. He was gentle while writing as any more than a little pressure would tear a hole in the napkins. He drew a map with extreme accuracy and began to draw lines which would be his route. With every line he drew he could almost feel the sea air blowing through his hair and the sound of waves crashing into the boat, and he began to picture all the locations he would soon be experiencing. A smile appeared as he was day dreaming of the adventures to come. The young lady who was serving him asked what he was doing – his words were short and sweet. He said, "Daring to live." Confused, the young lady left him to his napkins. After the young man had finished mapping out his route, he sat back in awe of what was to come. The wind picked up so he put the napkin in his pocket and ordered another cup of tea. For the first time for as long as the young man could remember, he had a plan and was excited for the days ahead. It was a weird feeling, not being uneasy or anxious about what he was going to do. He was sipping his tea, watching the world go by and was thinking of the old man while a cool breeze kept the air fresh.

On the walk back from the café, the young man passed people who were frantically rushing around, jumping into taxis, doing work on their lunch breaks, arguing on phones, or simply just sitting down glued to a device. He saw all this in black and white. In his eyes, he saw a world with little meaning and little purpose. He walked, with his mind taking in so much data that everything slowed down, everything was dark and gloomy. He saw the lives of these people and didn't recognise it; it was as if he was from another world.

Everything remained black and white until he saw Delilah, then colour returned and he saw meaning and purpose. As he went aboard and sat in the cabin, he thought about how some people were just not made for what society expected of them; some were built to wander and roam. Some people were the exception to the rule; some were renegades born for adventure. The young man smiled and whispered to himself, "I hope there are others like me; there must be."

Once the young man had finished with his thoughts, he started prepping for his travels – ordering equipment, food supplies and all the other essentials he would need for weeks at sea.

A few days went by. The young man spent his evenings watching the sun set and gazing up at the stars. He reread the old man's letter probably a hundred times; when he read it he felt close to the old man, as if he were still there with him.

The night before his adventure, he couldn't sleep. He just lay in bed, looking at the ceiling, thinking. He became anxious and went to the bathroom to splash cold water on his face, hopefully washing away the anxiety. Then he looked at himself in the mirror, with the water running down his face, and breathed, staring into his own eyes. He spent a few minutes focusing on his breath, then went back to bed. Through exhaustion, he fell asleep.

Today was the day, the day he was going to leave for the adventure of a lifetime. The finishing touch to a now beautifully restored boat, was a polaroid picture of the young man and the old man – proudly stuck in the cabin. The young man was now heading down the river, anxiously waiting to start his journey across the Atlantic. This would be his first time sailing alone, no old man sitting at the back with a watchful eye. He was nervous, but then the old man's voice came into his head saying, "The blood of Poseidon is in your veins." The nerves were still there but were channelled into excitement.

The young man began muttering to himself. He said, "Hopefully I will find myself, find some meaning to it all, find something I'm good at and something I can devote myself to or if not, have one hell of an adventure. And with a little luck, maybe both." He then took one last deep breath of London air and didn't look back.

Chapter 3

The young man had been at sea four days now. He had rather enjoyed himself so far and was getting use to sailing alone which was good as he would be crossing the Atlantic soon. Every time he got a little stressed or forgot what to do he took a deep breath and remembered the old man's words. As he was pulling the ropes or adjusting course, he had the old man's voice in his head keeping him calm, giving him instructions and talking him through it. But first, the young man would visit Lisbon, the coastal capital of Portugal, and he couldn't wait.

The young man sailed into Lisbon in the early hours of the morning, was filled with excitement and nerves. He had heard many of the old man's stories of travels and adventures but, now he was to live his own, he felt nervous. The young man moored up at one of Lisbon's many marinas,

He felt the history of Portuguese sea farers; it was like an invisible piece of art only he could see. The Portuguese were the ones to kick off the age of discovery and vast sea voyages. For many Portuguese, the sea is their lifeline and they are all connected to her through ancestors who braved the unknown. He thought about Delilah being moored up where ships of discovery could have once been, and how he and Delilah would discover the world together. He continued looking around the marina, thinking of ships that had once charted new routes on the ocean. All this thinking of discovery made the young man smile as he remembered the old man telling him stories of the explorer, Ernest Shackleton. The old man had grown up reading about Shackleton and his adventures and would a have twinkle in his eyes when talking about the age of brave exploration.

The young man then stepped off the deck and took his first real steps on his adventure. The second his feet touched Portuguese soil he felt different; those simple steps made him feel like a man and he felt reborn in that moment. Only a year ago he was a boy stuck in the city streets with no prospects and no vision of a better tomorrow, but now he was becoming a man and taking his first steps into an exciting new world.

The young man walked out of the marina and into the streets of Lisbon. He must have walked for miles before coming across the most picturesque road he had ever seen. Trams connected to the electrical lines above were moving up and down the road, which at one point converged in the middle. He continued to walk up this road until he could get a view of the sea; when high enough you could see the sea through the narrow gap of the street. Turning around, his view was postcard worthy. Graffiti covered a tram some of the walls on the buildings, red-tiled roofs were scattered in the distance, black cobbled streets contrasted with the stone cobbled paths. If you followed the tram wires above they guided your eyes down the road and into the sea. The young man took a few minutes to really look at this street. Ironically, he stopped where two big red stop signs were, the road almost telling him to stop and admire it.

After he had admired the road, he continued to walk the

streets of Lisbon. His belly started rumbling so he had lunch down a little road that he stumbled past. Quite a lot of Lisbon's most beautiful streets were cobbled and the young man found he liked it; his feet felt like they were transported back in time, to a time of horse and cart. He sat at a little table under colourful bunting that zig zagged across the buildings. He ordered an ice water and the day's special, then read some of his book.

While exploring the city, the young man found a bar which was a poetry venue; it was small and cosy with a little stage big enough for a stool and a microphone. He was welcomed in by a man who walked him to a table where there was an empty seat. This spiked the young man's anxiety and he instantly thought about running. But once he sat down he found that everyone was pleasant,, introduced themselves and welcomed him into their conversation, and his anxiety went away. During the conversation, the young man told them all that he had been writing a little and sometimes found poetry an easier way of communicating his emotions. His new friends encouraged him to read some of his poetry, telling him that poetry reflects your emotion and state of mind, so it can never be bad. But if, somehow, it didn't go well, they would all go out to forget about it so it didn't matter how it turned out. Someone at the table said, "No, no. No matter what, we shall go out and dance with the night; the night is young and it is our duty to show our new friend our beautiful city."

So, when a slot opened up, the young man slowly walked up onto the stage that squeaked when he stood on one of the wooden planks. He stood in front of the small but intimate crowd and adjusted the stool a little closer to the microphone; the sound of the dragging of the stool blasted through the speakers, silencing everyone in the room. Then the young man closed his eyes, trying to picture his diary with the words of the poem he had written not too long ago, and began to speak.

"I used to play in the devil's playground and sometimes I still do, I swing on his swings and slide down his slides, I would play with my demons, even when I was asleep we played. Round and round I go on his merry-go-round, spinning out of control, round and round, round and round I would go on his merry-go-round. My vision became blurry, days became weeks, weeks became years and years became one. I had died a thousand deaths in a thousand simulations in my mind, hoping and begging one would come true. I tried a simulation once. But the devil wouldn't let me leave his playground ... no, not me, he wasn't done with me yet. Round and round I went, back round his merry-go-round. But I was dragged out of the devil's playground by a silver knight, I still go back to the playground but now I dream, I dream in colour, I dream vividly of a better tomorrow, I had a dream for the first time and now I never want to stop. The simulations in my mind became simulations of possibilities not probabilities. I was no longer playing Russian roulette in my mind every day, hearing the clinking of the weapon of my thoughts that rested against my head, they no longer haunt me. Wait, that's a lie. They still do, waiting for me in the dark, but now they're more light than dark and I feel my veins carrying passion, desire, and hope around my body. I now play in a playground of my choosing."

When he had finished his poem, the young man began breathing heavily. It could be heard through the speakers, his nervous breath adding to the poem and the performance. After a few moments, he opened his eyes to a room filled with staring faces, shocked at his beautiful display of honesty, pure honesty. A few more moments passed and then they began clapping. His nerves disappeared, and his hand stopped shaking. He walked back to the table, still surrounded by the sounds of clapping, and sat down. His new friends were all smiling at him. They all had a few more drinks to celebrate the young man's moment, had more conversation and listened to more poetry. The young man had his picture taken and was put on the venue's Wall of Fame, there and then.

After the poetry reading ended, the group of people the young man had been sharing a table decided to head to a bar that sat on top of a multi-storey car park. Once they arrived, they all sat on wooden deckchairs on the rooftop overlooking the city. The view from the rooftop was truly something; the lights of the city glowed like the candle on their table.

One of them said, "I think the city is the most beautiful from up here."

The all continued talking together and with others. After an hour or so, someone said, "I'm bored now; let's go somewhere else."

"But where?"

"Let's just walk and see what the city gives us."

So they all got up, finished their drinks, and walked the Lisbon streets.. The young man's new friends gave him a tour of the city, all giving their own unique twist and perspectives on it. The city became more alive through their stories. The young man's first day of his adventure and his first day ever of being abroad couldn't have been better.

That night, the young man sat on the deck of the boat and watched the stars. He smiled as the boat rocked him from side to side. He got the old man's letter out and read it quietly out loud to himself. He thought about the words he had said to himself not even a week ago while going down the river as he made his way out to sea. "Hopefully I will find myself, find some meaning to it all, find something I'm good at and can devote myself to or, if not, have one hell of an adventure. And with a little luck, maybe both." He thought about how he was on the right path for it all to come true and this comforted his fragile mind.

The next day the young man ventured out to the streets of Lisbon again. A little later in the day, he met a street performer in a little café. He had been playing outside and came in for lunch. The café was small, only big enough for three tables and a long bench that stretched the length of the window. While waiting at the counter, they began a little small talk. The young man was unsure about what to order and the performer had suggested his favourite item off the menu, Bacalhau à Brás. He said it was heaven and comfort in a bowl, and the young man thought eating heaven and comfort sounded nice.

Once the young man had ordered his bowl of comfort food, he sat down looking out of the window onto the street. Then he heard a voice saying, "Mind if I join you?" Before the young man could respond or even know who was talking to him, the performer had sat down. He introduced himself as Marco. They ate lunch together and spoke about a little bit of everything. The young man asked Marco where he found the confidence to do what he did. "How do you sing on the street in front of all those people?"

Marco told the young man he had a gig later in a club nearby and said, "You're going to sing a song on stage with me."

The young man laughed but Marco didn't.

"Oh, you're not joking!" the young man said. "I can't do that! I could barely say a poem in a room with about twenty people in; I nearly had a panic attack." ,

"You will be fine," said Marco. "We have the day to prepare you."

For some unknown reason, the young man agreed to Marco's idea, but then asked, "How many people will be at this gig?"

Marco smiled and said, "You will just have to wait and see."

, As they walked the Lisbon streets Marco suddenly stopped and started dancing. The young man was embarrassed but Marco said, "Come and dance with me!" The young man shook his head but Marco told him, "You need to stop caring what other people are thinking. Let go of the embarrassment and let go of the fear." Marco, now fed up with the young man's stubbornness, pulled him out and made him dance. "Let go . Just let go."

So the young man closed his eyes and let go. Marco stood to the side and started stamping his feet on the ground and clapping his hands, making a beat for the young man. He had just jumped the first hurdle and Marco now had to stop him letting go.

They talked more while exploring the city together; they looked at buildings, people, monuments. Marco made the young man laugh at how he saw the city and the way he saw everything really.

Marco saw a group of young adults and told the young man they were going to go and dance and sing in front of them. Laughing and turning around while walking away, the young man said, "No, that one is too far."

Marco ran in front of him, stopping him in his tracks, and he said, "I'm going over there and you can join me or watch me. Either way, I'm going and letting go – confidence is a choice."

When he got to the group, he started playing air guitar. The young man stood there fighting with himself, then said, "Screw it!" He ran over and joined Marco. He and Marco were laughed at but they didn't care; they were in that moment together.

After they had finished, they bowed to their not-so-adoring fans and walked off, laughing at themselves and what they had just done. The young man's heart was racing and adrenaline was coursing through his veins. Marco smiled at him, was surprised he had it in him. They then got coffee from a food truck and sat on a bench overlooking the Padrão dos Descobrimentos, a monument to Portuguese exploration. After sipping at their coffees and looking at the monument, Marco said, "I still get anxious and nervous when I do gigs or any other kind of performance. I just say screw it and tell myself I'm confident, positive affirmations. You tell yourself you're confident, you'll begin to feel confident."

The young man smiled and said, "I'll try."

Marco shook his head. "You still don't get it. Don't just try, do!"

They both walked back to his apartment to get ready for the gig tonight. A few hours passed and the young man was introduced to Marco's friends and band members as they all relaxed in the apartment before they had to leave.

As they walked into the venue, the young man tapped Marco on the shoulder. "There's hundreds of people here!"

"I know, isn't it exciting?"

The young man then walked through the crowds to get backstage and on the way, he muttered, "Exciting? Try terrifying!"

Backstage the young man was getting anxious. Soon Marco and his friends were called up on stage. The young man hung back, waiting for his signal. Marco told the crowd to be nice. The young man was waved on stage; he took a shot of something and said screw it as he walked up a few steps. Once on stage, a microphone was placed in front of him and the band began playing. Marco started the song off but when it was his turn, he froze. The band quickly adapted and started the song again. Marco stood next to the young man and said, "Let go, just let go."

He took a deep breath and began singing. The young man was completely tone deaf; his voice was awful but the crowd didn't mind. They cheered him on and when he heard this, his confidence grew and he unleashed his inner performer. Marco and his friends all surrounded the young man and, cheek to cheek, they all sung their hearts out.

The young man walked off stage, buzzing, as if he had just been electrocuted with life; he had never felt anything like that before. When Marco and his friends came off stage, they all ran over to the young man, picking him up and hugging him. Marco said, "You just sang in front of all those people!" On this amazing high, they partied the night away, listening to all the other bands that braved the stage, jumping in sync with everyone in the crowd.

The night ended and Marco and his friends dropped the young man off at the marina. As they continued their walk home, the young man could still hear them all singing when they were out of view. Once he was back aboard Delilah, he sat on the side of the boat with his feet hanging over the side, leaning on the handrail looking out to sea. The young man enjoyed moments of solitude; they provided clarity and the perfect environment for wondering thoughts.

In the early morning, the young man danced out of the marina, coffee in one hand and earphones in. He sat on the wall waiting for Marco and his friends to arrive. As he waited, he was swinging and kicking his legs in rhythm to the music.

CHAPTER 3

A couple of songs later they arrived. A van pulled up and the side door was pulled open. For a second the young man thought he was going to be kidnapped, but it was just Marco who jumped out with a smile on his face, hitting the side door in excitement to see him. The young man jumped in and had a harness thrown at him.

"What's this for?" he asked.

The driver looked into his rear-view mirror at the young man and said, "We're going climbing!" He smiled, looking out at the road ahead with the wind blowing in through the windows, music nearly blowing the speakers ...

They arrived at the beach and made their way to the wall. Once there, they did a few smaller climbs to teach the young man what he needed to know and so they could all warm up. Then one of the friends tied himself in the harness and began climbing, making sure to attach the rope to the carabiners on the way up. The first friend's arms got tired so they lowered him down and then the next one went up ...

The young man sat on a rock and watched. He was trying to figure out a route for himself; he didn't want to fall off straight away. He looked at how they were climbing, the way they moved, when they took breaks, the way they gripped the rocks, when they stopped for chalk – every little detail.

The young man was up next, so he put his hands in the chalk bag he had been given. Rubbing his hands together, he made the chalk fall down on him like snow and left little white speckles all over him. He took grip of the rock face and was about to start climbing as someone behind him, he thought it was Marco, said, "Remember, just breath and have fun ..."

So, the young man began to climb up the rock face with a little guidance from below. He had climbed higher than they expected and with an ease that was empowering and yet quite annoying at the natural skill he possessed. Once he got to the hard part of the climb, the belayer supported him while he sat back off the wall for a break. He sat back for a moment to look up the wall, seeing if there was a route he could take. He also tried looking for chalk marks from people who'd gone before ... Before climbing up again, he took a moment and looked out to sea with the sun on his face, all the while taking a deep breath, energizing himself.

After reaching into the rear pouch and getting a little more chalk on his hands, he continued climbing. He got a little higher before a voice below told him he was going to have to jump for the next hold. Only one of the friends had managed this part of the climb today. He took a deep breath and then made the leap of faith. His stomach tightened as he began to fall and then he crashed into the wall. A voice from below said, "Nice try. We'll lower you down now." He got to the bottom, now battered and bruised but still smiling.

They spent all day doing this, rotating from the sea to the wall and when they weren't doing either of these, they were laying on blankets as the rocks were scorching, talking and resting their arms. Marco and his friends began asking the young man about his route.

"Won't it be a little hard going for you to sail alone?"

The young man replied with a devilishly optimistic smile and said, "Yes, it will, but me and the old man use to go out in bad weather, well, I say we use to go out, he made us go out. He told me, 'you'll only ever be a real sailor if you've looked a storm in the eye'."

Chapter 4

The young man had now been at sea two days since leaving Portugal. The coast was nowhere to be seen; there was only blue ocean everywhere. The first two days back at sea were hard – big swells and huge downpours of rain, the seawater washed over the deck – and for those two days the young man remained wet despite wearing waterproofs. He began to question why he was on the trip and why he had glorified the journey in his mind so much. The old man had prepared him for the journey; he had purposely woken the young man up when he knew bad weather was due, always saying "the real training starts today". But to sail these barbaric waves without the old man was different, it felt more intense and at times a little lonely. The young man didn't normally get seasick but these swells would make anyone a little queasy. He hadn't washed yet, the hair on his head was salty, the same for the skin on his face. Although the sun was nowhere to be seen, his face was red, mostly the end of his nose and cheeks. He had been battered by the elements, but he had made it through in one piece.

By the third day, the weather had calmed and the sun shone. He was en route to the Caribbean, specifically the tiny island of Jamaica. The old man had shown him pictures; an archaic polaroid showed the young man the tropical paradise and ever since the old man had shown him the picture, he had craved the island. The young man vigorously checked his course every hour; the old man had taught him militaristic discipline when it came to navigation. While he wasn't sailing the boat, he lay on the wooden decking of the boat reading one of the vast amount of books the old man had collected and writing a diary. The old man's one condition for the young man to write in a diary was probably one of the old man's greatest gifts. The young man had fallen in love with the relationship he formed with pen and paper. The young man loved being able to clear his mind, by putting his thoughts and ideas on paper; it provided him clarity and a form of expression. Every day without question, the young man watched the sunset and stared in astonishment at the night sky; the old man had told him he could find him there, so the young man did find him there each day. This was one of the young man's favourite times of day. On day six of his Atlantic crossing, the young man had found himself a friend; a dolphin. The dolphin was a beautiful iron grey with a white spot around its left eye. The most unique feature of this majestic creature was a long scar on its back; it wasn't a nice clean cut line it was ragged and coarse looking. The young man liked to think his new friend was a hero, and the scar was a mark of bravery defending a damsel in distress from some evil illegal poachers. The dolphin had been following him for about two days now, in his diary he wrote:

"I've made a friend, an elegant dolphin I've decided to name Charlie, who I found out today loves to show off with the most spectacular dives and flips - Charlie even comes up to the boat. I rubbed its nose and managed to play fetch with him today. I had an old volleyball on the boat so I used that to throw. After it's had enough, it swims off in spectacular fashion. I do wonder what it would be like to be a dolphin – no worries of the human sort, imagine that. I do love the sea and my isolation upon it, it provides a clarity found nowhere else, a tranquillity like no other. I have also started to wonder why this boat is called Delilah. I never did ask the old man. Anyway, the sun is due to set and I do love to see it drop below the horizon and then the glittering darkness of the moonlit sea."

The young man was now a day's sailing away from Jamaica but he wasn't sure what he would do upon his arrival. He thought he would just get lost and explore the island. The day's sailing had passed by quickly and before the young man could explore the island, he had to stop off in Port Antonio and do the boring paperwork side of sailing around the world. He waited patiently on the deck of his boat for a port authority officer to grant him his visa and provide him with the much-loved paperwork he had been waiting for.

He set off again and sailed down to Boston Bay; it was only a short trip. As the young man dropped anchor off the coast, he took the in view from the deck of Delilah: the deep greens of the forest, golden beaches, all the colours amazed the young man and his eyes didn't know where to look; his eyes bounced around the landscape in front of him. He slipped his flippers on and dived into the sea with a dry bag strapped to his back. He made the swim and landed on the warm golden beaches of Boston Bay. As he walked along the beach, flippers in one hand, sea water dripping off him, brushing his fingers through his salty brown hair, he saw a beach shack with some tables outside; it looked like a restaurant. As he went in, he was welcomed by a very charming man.

"Hey, man, how can I help?"

The young man said he would like something to eat.

"Sorry, the kitchen's closed now; the cook's gone home. This your first time on the island?"

The young man said, "Yes, how did you know?"

"Just a feeling. The name's Eithan, by the way." He came out from behind the counter and went to shake the young man's hand.

They sat outside, feet in the sand and got talking. Not too long into the conversation, Eithan had a good feeling about the young man and said, "You can have dinner with me and my family, if you like. It's not far from here. My wife's one of the best cooks on the island."

The young man had never met someone so welcoming and trusting. As they walked to Eithan's home, they began talking about this and that.

"Nice boat by the way," said Eithan. "I saw you coming from the beach."

The young man said, "You should come aboard sometime. We can go on a little trip.".

"Maybe," Eithan said.

They arrived at Eithan's house which was hidden by an almost fortified wall of trees. The house was an explosion of colour; each wall was a different colour – bright blues, greens, yellows, and reds! Surfboards were standing up against the wall. The young man and Eithan had dinner with the family. Eithan's wife had coked fresh fish over the fire. Simple but devilishly good, it had the most exotic flavours the young man had ever tasted. When he asked her for the recipe, Eithan burst out laughing, saying, "I'm not even allowed to know!" She just gave a smile and the young man new she wasn't going to tell him a thing, he would just have to come back for more. After dinner, the young

CHAPTER 4

man and Eithan strolled onto the front porch and sat on the doorstep talking. He told him about the old man, the night of the bridge and his journey so far. Eithan told him about growing up on the island and mostly his love for surfing.. Eithan was going to give him his first lesson the next day at dawn, as that was the best time to surf.

The young man went back to his boat before the sun set; he didn't fancy making the swim back in the dark. As he dragged himself aboard, he sat at the back of the boat on a little ledge close to the water's surface with his feet in the water making small swirls, watching the sunset. Later that night he sat and stared at the stars with a cold beer, compliments of Eithan who had slipped it into his dry bag on the beach. He then laid in the hammock he had set up on the deck, gently swaying side to side as the waves rocked the boat ever so calmly. He fell asleep under the stars, with his book gently resting on his chest.

He woke to the sound of a loud voice saying, "What you doing sleeping, man? The day's already started." It was Eithan on his surfboard next to the boat. The young man swung out of the hammock, still half asleep, rubbing the sleep dust out of his eyes. He leaned over the side of the boat to talk to Eithan, but he had already begun to ride a wave to shore. The young man watched intently as Eithan gracefully glided over the waves; for a few moments it was almost slow motion – as if time had frozen for that very wave. The young man then rushed to put his flippers on, dived into the crystal waters of Boston Bay and landed on the beach for his first lesson.

When he made it ashore Eithan joked and said, "You took your time." He then had the young man practising jumping up on the board on the beach and while he was doing that, he provided instructions on what to expect next when on the waves.

Eventually he decided to throw him in the deep end, so they paddled out to find a wave. When Eithan felt the time was right he said, "Go man."

The young man paddled hard, going over his surfing 101 crash course in his head. Then, as the wave began to form, he jumped up, landed on the board and for a few moments felt like he was a surfer, only to majestically tumble into the waves. Eithan sat on his board giggling. "Wipe out!" Eithan then rode the next wave in his elegantly slow-motion way. As he glided to shore, the young man crawled there with a face that was not too happy.

"I quit! Don't think surfing's my thing," he said.

A long silence filled the air. Eithan looking at the young man and said, "We fall so we can rise."

"I don't want to fall," the young man said.

"We must fall, and we will all fall; only the courageous continue to stand up."

A few seconds passed. Eithan picked up his board, paddled out a little and then faced the young man, saying, "A tree cannot grow to heaven unless its roots reach down to hell." Eithan then paddled off. The young man had just learned his first lesson of many to come.

He sank to his knees, pondering his next decision, but more so pondering what Eithan had just said to him. He didn't really understand but knew it was profound and to learn more he would have to get back on the board. So, he did. He picked up his board and he paddled out. He came alongside Eithan sat up on his board and said, "Tell me more, please. What did you mean by heaven and hell?"

"In time. We surf first," Eithan said.

They then spent the rest of the morning surfing, well, lots

CHAPTER 4

of tumbling and crashing for the young man, but he was improving fast, Eithan thought. He wasn't going to tell the young man, though; didn't want to inflate his ego.

After a morning of surfing, both the young man and Eithan were starving, so they carried their boards ashore and put them in the back of ' 4x4. They went to a small café in the centre of town, about a ten minute drive from the beach. As they drove into the centre of town, Eithan was waving and saying hello to everyone walking by; even if he didn't know them, he would say hello. Before they got into the 4x4, Eithan had warned the young man that the door sometimes randomly popped open. He usually kept it shut by tying the sea belt around it. The young man said, "I'll just hold the door closed." Ten minutes later they walked into the cafe that had concrete floors and walls with paint-stripped wooden windows overlooking the town square. The windows were a baby blue and just outside the window, next to the table the young man and Eithan were sitting at, was a view of the colonial town square with a market full of traders trading, buyers buying and a group of men were playing dominoes on tables set up on the grass next to the market. The café also had pictures of Jamaican athletes all over the bare walls; the owner was a proud Jamaican and loved any sport that represented his beloved country. The walls were a collage of Jamaican success. As the young man and Eithan waited for their lunch to be cooked, Eithan was about to tell the young man what he meant by "a tree cannot grow to heaven unless its roots reach down to hell."

Eithan said to the young man, "While I was at university, I studied psychology and loved it, and during my studies I came across a man named Carl Jung – that's where I found the heaven and hell quote. I took that quote and put my own spin on what it means." Eithan took a pause to gather his thoughts, then continued to tell the young man, "what it means can simply be explained as light and dark, ying and yang, sun and moon. The point is, if you want success you must embrace failure; if you want happiness you must embrace sadness; if you want to stand you must embrace falling; if you don't want to suffer you have to embrace suffering. Success and happiness only mean what they do because of their opposites. If you take away one, you end up taking away both. Failure is success' best friend; failure is the best teacher to achieve long term success. That's why I said you must prepare to fall while learning to surf, as falling will allow you to stand. So, heaven is success and happiness and hell is failure and sadness, but we will never grow without both in our lives."

The young man smiled and said he now understood. Lunch then promptly arrived. Eithan had ordered an array of traditional Jamaican dishes; the waiter had to pull over another table as they'd ordered so much. This brought much attention to them in the cafe as the waiters had to pull over yet another table to fit all the food on. They spoke for hours in that cafe and after they had finished eating, they moved outside to sit at one of the tables that lined the street. Eventually Eithan had to go home, so he drove the young man back to the beach and said he would see him for tomorrow's lesson.

A few days had passed now, lots of surfing and the young man and Eithan had even ventured out on a little road trip to explore the island with Eithan's family. They drove in rhis raggedy convertible 4X4, driving along the coast blasting out reggae from one of the very few things working on the vehicle – the speakers. They were heading for Falmouth. Eithan told the young man he had a surprise for him later.

CHAPTER 4

The drive took a few hours, so the young man had plenty of time to take in the scenery with the reggae feeding his soul. About thirty minutes into the journey the kids had fallen asleep. "I think I bored them; they fell asleep while I was talking," the young man joked. The kids had curled up next to the young man on the back seats, both using each other as a pillow. Now all the young man had to do was take mental photographs of this stunning country. He liked taking photographs but being in the moment and just having the memory of it was, in his opinion, better than any photograph; you can close your eyes and live the moment over and over again.

They soon arrived in Falmouth where they met up with Eithan's uncle who was a fisherman. They ate together at the marina. The uncle had prepared dinner for them – fish he had caught earlier that day was on the menu and was nearly ready upon their arrival. They sat at a table overlooking the marina. The uncle liked the young man as they were both men of the sea and loved his stories of crossing the Atlantic alone. As the sun set over the bay, they all got their chairs right up to the water's edge and watched it drop below the horizon.

"Right, you ready for the surprise?" Eithan said.

"Yes," said the young man eagerly.

They all got into the uncle's boat (the wife made sure the kids were wearing life jackets) and as they made their way out of the marina, one of Eithan's children took the young man's hand and said, "You're going to love this." He smiled and a few moments later the young man had no words. His jaw dropped to the bottom of the bay. The sea turned neon blue around the boat as it moved through the water; the young man thought Eithan's uncle must have put something in the fish.

Eithan came over and put his arm around the young man who

was lost in the water and said, "It amazes me every time. The earth has so much beauty. You only have to turn around and she will provide you with something to be amazed by. There's probably a scientific reason for the electric colours but I like to think Mother Nature has blessed this water with beauty, like she put a little bit of extra attention into this part of the world."

They continued to move through the water and when they got to a spot they knew well, they all jumped out. As they swam around the lit up water, the young man couldn't believe what he was seeing. The moon was out and the water was neon; he had to keep reminding himself it wasn't a dream.

Once they had finished swimming they all climbed back aboard and, once dried off, the kids had fallen asleep hugging Eithan, one on each shoulder. They all sat talking as the boat now made its way back to shore. The young man kept looking out at the water. He put his hand in the water as the boat was moving, the neon water rushing through his fingers.

The young man climbed up to the upper deck and was welcomed by a pat on the back. The uncle said to the young man, "You in love with her yet?"

The young man, a little confused, said, "Who?"

"Jamaica, of course!"

He then smiled and told the uncle, "I fell in love with her the moment I saw her."

The uncle smiled too. They then talked. The young man told him in greater detail about his Atlantic crossing. The uncle loved his stories and he told the young man a little about himself and how he became a fisherman.

"When I was a child, I worked for a fisherman to get some money. I helped him after school. Eventually I was going out on the boat with him and I fell in love with the ocean; the waves and the ocean fulfilled me. I was lucky, I suppose, finding what I loved, but it doesn't mean it wasn't hard work. While working for the fisherman, I saved every penny I had to buy my own boat. When I had enough and bought it, I had no money left. I had taken a risk and again, luckily for me, it paiofd off, Day after day I got fish and now all these years later I'm still here." The young man sat on the chair next to him wanting to hear more. The uncle said, "I don't have any fancy advice for you, like my nephew, but I'll leave you with this … Play the cards you're given the best you can."

They spoke for a little longer then the young man climbed back down to the lower level and sat with a smile on his face, watching the waves form behind the boat. They spent the night in Falmouth and in the morning Eithan, the uncle and the young man went surfing. The sun hadn't quite risen yet but the sky was warm. As they walked to the beach, Eithan said, "You think I'm good, then watch him. He's been surfing for forty years now."

All three of them glided over the waves. The young man looked at Eithan and gave a nod, letting Eithan know he agreed, the uncle was amazing. After they'd finished surfing, they sat on their boards, looked out to sea and watched the sun rise. They then paddled ashore and made their way back to the uncle's house before the young man and Eithan's family made their way back home; it was only a quick visit as they all had to go back to work. The drive back was the same as the one there – the kids fell asleep on each other and the stereo played reggae with the views of the ocean to complement it. Once they got back, the young man and Eithan went for a walk. The young man's time on the island was coming to an end; he had only one night left. They walked through the town; the food stalls created smoke screens which acted like doors to enter the next enchanting area.

As they walked through the market with sounds of food cooking, people haggling, and the clambering of footsteps, the young man put one arm around Eithan. He laid his head on his shoulder and thanked him for everything he'd done. Eithan just said, "No worries." They then continued the walk through the market and the streets, and ended the day at a beach bar for a farewell send-off where Eithan's wife and some friends were waiting. The night was filled with rum, lots of rum! And singing and dancing – the young man was not a dancer, but anyone can dance after rum and reggae music and I mean, anyone. The bar was small and only lit by fairy lights and a few neon signs behind the bar. The beach was the dance floor and the stage for rum-fuelled performances. The young man and Eithan ended the night in the early hours of the next day. They watched the sunrise together and then the time came to say farewell.

The young man smiled and said, "I don't want to go."

"You must go on, my friend; you must go on your journey," Eithan replied. "And you won't be gone – Jamaica will never leave you. It has left its mark on you and our friendship shall live as long as the stars, my friend." They hugged. The young man handed Eithan a picture of them both from the beach, the two of them standing next to their boards. On the back, he simply wrote, "A tree cannot grow to heaven unless its roots reach down to hell." Eithan put his hand over his heart and gave the young man a nod. He had something for the young man, it was a Rastafarian flag, which the young man loved. Eithan's wife bought over a surf-board, and Eithan said, "This is the real gift. You're going to need one, as the next time we see each other I expect you to be hitting all the big waves." The young man smiled and couldn't get the words out that he wanted, but managed to get out a "thank you". Eithan saw the other words in the young man's eyes.

The young man's adventure in Jamaica was now over and he set sail once again. with Eithan and his wife waving him off into the distance, he looked back and smiled at what he had and then looked out towards the horizon and smiled at what was to come.

Chapter 5

A little over a month had passed since Jamaica and Eithan. The young man had been hopping between the Caribbean islands, from Cuba to what the young man called the stepping-stone islands that started at the British Virgin Islands and finished in Grenada. While hopping between the islands he was perfecting his sailing and surfing, and immersing himself in the local culture. He was now infatuated and in a deep romance with travel and Delilah, his boat. The young man had bought a spear gun on one of the islands and thought he'd try to catch his own fish and cook it on the grill. He was hoping, with a little luck, to try to replicate Eithan's wife's recipe.

He was now en route to Brazil. He could not wait, as he found South American culture mesmerising. The old man had been there; he had been to the carnival and the stories he had told the young man! There was a picture of the old man and Ruby at the carnival from decades ago; they were both being kissed on the cheek by two performers with an explosion of colour going on behind them. The young man needed to experience it for himself. He had three weeks until he needed to be in Rio for the carnival; he crossed off each day on a little calendar in the kitchen.

CHAPTER 5

He spent the next three weeks going down the Brazilian coast. He rented 4x4s in every place he went and took road trips inland, sometimes with a guide and sometimes without, as he wanted to be alone so he could get lost – he believed that some of the best places you went were often by mere chance. The young man would spend his evenings with locals, dancing, drinking, and telling stories, and he would never miss a sunset. The young man had quickly realised on his travels so far that yes, the destinations you visit are beautiful and captivating, but the most beautiful thing about a destination are the people you meet and the memories forged with the culture.

The young man's journey south had been pleasant; the weather was kind and made sailing fun. He sometimes got carried away with getting to the next destination and he would forget to enjoy the simple pleasures that sailing provided, like the wind rushing through his hair, his morning coffee on the deck or racing along the coast when the winds picked up and he skimmed over the waves. But the young man was good at reminding himself of the simple pleasures; he just had to be mindful and stay in the moment.

The young man was a day's sailing away from Rio, and in the evening of that day, as the boat swayed side to side and the sun made the sea glitter, he pondered about what the carnival would be like. The old man had told him stories, so the young man closed his eyes and imagined. His image was in black and white (In his mind, the all the old man's stories were in black and white. This may have been due to the old man's age.). He envisaged a great parade with men and women dancing everywhere, the parade well synchronised, almost militaristic in its precision, yet graceful in it's display. With explosions of light, his imagination limited his vision. Maybe It didn't want to ruin what was going to be a life-changing experience. He opened his eyes and watched the sunset with the lush Brazilian coast next to him.

The day had come. The young man sailed into Rio. Before arriving at the marina, he saw the city through the gaps in the mountains. As he got closer and made his way into the harbour the city grew before his eyes and soon enough he was in the marina. He carefully tied up Delilah, picked up his bag and went to explore the streets of Rio. As soon as he looked up, his eyes locked onto Christ the Redeemer and the vast mountain tops. He stood in pure wonder. His body wouldn't let him move; all focus was on this mesmerising figure. This was by far the most beautiful and astonishing sight the young man had seen so far, the giant figure almost welcoming you into Rio's loving arms.

As his body came out of its wonderment, he left the marina and went out to explore the city. The day was filled with lots of food, a trip to a museum and what was the young man's favourite part of the day – he took a taxi to Little Africa which was a cultural fusion at its finest. He went to what is considered the birthplace of the carnival: Pedra do Sal. The young man's favourite part of Little Africa was Salt Rock Alley. A local man told him that it was called this because many years ago slaves used to carry salt from ships up the rock so it could be distributed around the country. The very steps he was walking were carved out by the slaves themselves; he could feel the history underneath his feet. He was captured by the art in Salt Rock Valley; nearly every wall in every direction was covered in street art. Once the young man was finished exploring, he found a little restaurant to have a bite in before getting a taxi back to the marina and the comfort of Delilah.

It was the night of the carnival. The young man waited eagerly

CHAPTER 5

for the parade to start. As it came closer, the young man was hit by a tsunami of colour and giant floats. The first was a huge bird with a giant golden beak, purple and blue feathers. It was captivating and the attention to detail was remarkable. It had a lifelike presence; you almost expected it to take off and fly into the night sky. This float was surround by the most beautiful dancers moving in a flow-like state, only comparable to the waves of the sea moving in unpredictable unison. The parade made him feel euphoric, as if he was in another dimension- The young man had no worries; he was complete immersed in the spectacle. The parade had instantaneously put him in a state of joy and happiness, as all around him people were dancing, smiling and laughing with loved ones and even people they had just met. It was a celebration of life and you celebrated with everyone. Each float different from the last, all intrinsically beautiful and charismatic. One float was made to look like the amazon rainforest, a lush green float with huge pink, blue and yellow flowers around it. At first, they looked just like flowers, but with a second glance he realised they were performers, moving as if the wind was carrying them. The float was surrounded by dancers dressed up as animals of the forest, moving and shifting between each other, all in character, not breaking it even for a second. One dancer was a predator prowling around the float – the animalistic reality of his movements almost sent shivers down your spine. If you watched for a second too long, you felt like theatrical prey.

The young man was now engrossed in this dazzling spectacle. All his senses were super charged sending messages to the brain saying, 'WE LOVE THIS'. They all worked in harmony to create an everlasting. Then just when it seemed it couldn't get any better, the fireworks went off; the night sky was pitch black and a split second later it erupted with the most vibrant light, scattered across the night sky. The floats continued to come, with an army of performers dancing under the night sky. The floor seemed to rattle to the sound of the music.

The parade made the young man feel as if he had been living blind but now could see. The continuous flow of colour and light was all the performers performing as if it were their last dance, their last show, their last chance to perform, as if it were all to end tomorrow. There was so much colour, so much light, so much energy. For a second, he imagined being on the moon, sitting on the old man's three-legged chair, looking through a telescope watching the carnival.

As the night went on, the young man met a group of locals. He partied all night with them until the morning sun rose. They danced in the streets of Rio engulfed in the colours. He must have hugged and danced with over a hundred people. He loved the carnival all of Rio was the party every person and place was full of life. It was exhilarating and the atmosphere fuelled the soul.

The young man had gone back to his new friends' apartment later in the night or was it early morning? The neighbours all shared a communal garden which was lit up by bulbs hanging inside whiskey bottles and dangling from wires above. The bottles swung whenever somebody bumped into the wire they were tied up with. All the neighbours and friends were there, and they all drank and partied like there was no tomorrow. The carnival had injected a sense of passion and happiness the young man had never felt before. It was living and breathing in the night air. The young man talked to the most interesting people who all had stories which could be turned into a Hollywood movie. The young man smiled; these were the kind of experiences the

CHAPTER 5

old man had told him about on the deck of Delilah and the kind of experiences he had been craving.

It was now two days after the carnival. The young man had spent the following day with his new friends and their neighbours. They were nursed back to health by some good cooking which they shared on the rooftop overlooking the city, reminiscing over the carnival. But today the young man was going into the favelas to volunteer with local children. He had met a man, Raphael, at the party a couple of nights ago. He ran a small youth charity called 'Voice to the People'. They helped the youth in the favelas through education programs, activities and by just being a caring mentor for the kids.

He was picked up by Raphael and as the young man sat in the backseat of his new friend's 4x4 looking out the window into the derelict looking streets of the favelas, he saw children playing football using bottle crates as goal posts. When one of the children scored a goal, all their teammates jumped in the air as if they had just won the world cup, the other team of kids sinking to their knees and throwing their arms up in disappointment. As he continued to look out the window he noticed people staring at the 4x4 as they drove past. He saw mounds of rubbish in the streets that people were walking by on their daily commutes and he saw the tin-roof shacks of homes for thousands. As they continued driving, the tin roofs seemed to grow up the mountain side; they really stood out to the young man as the orange of the bricks clashed with the greens of Rio's mountains. The young man was shocked that even in dire poverty, these children had hope and happiness.

The blurry whizzing of the view from the window allowed the young man a moment to ponder. But soon they arrived, and children surrounded the car with wide-eyed smiles. They spent the day painting murals in the small concrete football court which, before painting began, looked like it had been bombarded by a military airstrike. When the painting was done it became a mental sanctuary for the kids; they had a revitalised place to live. They also spent time playing games with the children; football was the most popular game of choice and all the kids laughed at the young man's non-existent football skills. They also laughed at the young man speaking to them in Spanish. The young man could speak fairly good Spanish but his conversations with the children were half understood at best as they spoke to him in Portuguese. This led to much laughter from the kids and awkward smiles from the young man as he waited to see if what he said was understood.

After the young man returned from the favelas, he sat in his hammock and couldn't stop thinking about the kids he had just spent the day with. He looked up and saw his surfboard on top of the cabin and a smile appeared. He knew what he could do for the kids. He would bring the group of them to the beach for the day and teach them to surf and paddleboard; most of the kids had never been to the beach or even in the sea. So later on in the evening he rang Raphael, the charity leader and told him the idea. He loved it and so they started planning it.

Raphael came over to the young man's boat. They had beers and the young man cooked for him. They planned it for two days from now and the young man became a little anxious as he knew he had to teach the kids how to surf. He remembered how his beloved friend Eithan had taught him, but these were kids; he couldn't throw them in the deep end so he spent the night coming up with a lesson plan. He went over and over it in his head, while also practising teaching. Anyone looking at him would have thought he was crazy as he was jumping up on

CHAPTER 5

his board and pretending to paddle while on his board was on the deck of his boat.

The morning arrived. The young man met up with the volunteers and once again they drove through the favela streets. This time the young man was less anxious as he was familiar with the cracked and crumbly buildings that were intertwined with a web of wires above. They arrived at the now beautifully decorated football court with all the kids waiting patiently. The young man jumped out of the minibus and started high fiving all the kids. Raphael got out his clipboard and started calling out names ...

"Gabriella."

"Here."

"Jose."

"Here."

"Diego."

"Here."

He continued to call out the names. All the kids had arrived apart from one, Antonio. Everyone piled onto the bus while the young man and Raphael waited outside; they were going to wait a few minutes for Antonio and, just as they said they were going, they heard a little voice shouting in the distance. They couldn't make out the words but Raphael smiled, laughed and shook his head. Before he could say anything a little figure came charging round the corner.

"WAIT!" he screamed while panting for air.

The young man and Raphael laughed. The little man ran onto the bus, all his friends cheering. The young man closed the sliding door. On the way to the beach, they picked up a few other volunteers who would be joining them: David from South Africa and Jessica from Canada.

As they drove to the beach, David started telling the young man and the others a story about his father and why he had chosen to dedicate his life to helping others. His story started as a young boy in Cape Town, South Africa. Growing up, his father would tell him an old Zulu proverb. "Umuntu ngumuntu ngabanye." It means every human being thrives as a human being because others thrive as human beings.

David said, "This proverb has been passed down and embraced by our family for generations."

He continued to tell them about his father growing up during the apartheid, and how awful it was, but David didn't really want to tell them about the negative experiences his father had had and the experiences he himself had endured. He wanted to tell them about the little pockets of light that appeared during his father's experiences of the apartheid and how this proverb injected meaning and hope into the world. His grandad had told David's father this proverb growing up and it had a profound effect on his life. David's father led a small group of people that helped his community and many other communities. He would help by getting people in the community to help each other with money troubles, food, childcare and anything else people needed. David's father integrated this proverb into the community as a way of life. Instead of people fending for themselves and suffering, everyone looked out for each other and life became a little easier and more meaningful in an environment that bred hate and suffering. David's father was a symbol of hope; he showed his and many other communities that the burdens of life that weigh us down can become but a feather when rested on many shoulders. 'Umuntu ngumuntu ngabanye' – I thrive because you thrive, you thrive because I thrive. David's father lived by this proverb and now David lived by it. He told the young man and the others that his father peacefully passed, surrounded by a loving community. It was a sad yet happy ending to what was an amazing life lived by an amazing man. On his death bed, David's father told him, "If throughout your life you can truly help but one person, it will make the world a better place. If everyone helped one person then think of the possibilities. I love you my son. Umuntu ngumuntu ngabanye."

David told the young man and the others, "I now travel the world trying to spread this proverb. I am on a noble crusade wherever I go. I want to continue my father's legacy and his father's and hopefully one day my children will want the same ... I was a curious child and in school our classroom had a map on the back wall. The world was so big on the map and even bigger in real life, I would later find out. When I would come home I would tell my father and mother about all the adventures I would go on one day. My father would always tell me that I could see it all if I wanted to. He told me home is where the heart is and no matter where you are, me and the family will love you."

The beach was in sight now and all the kids in the back had their faces glued to the window, all of them on top of each other, all trying to get a look at what was the most beautiful and freeing sight they had ever seen. They had been very noisy on the way but when they saw the sea they all went quite, not one sound. The young man and the volunteers looked back at them and smiled. They thought how magical it must be to be freed from a mental prison.

They arrived at the beach, all the kids sat and stared at the horizon. They were also struck by the beauty of Christ the Redeemer, just as the young man had been when he arrived in Rio. While the young man and the volunteers unloaded the surfboards and got everything ready, the kids played in the ocean under the watchful eye of David. The surfboards were lined up facing the ocean. The kids came running in from the ocean, dripping wet with salty hair. The young man taught the children in the same way Eithan had taught him –paddling on the beach and jumping up on the boards. But unlike Eithan, the young man wasn't going to throw the kids in at the deep end. He taught them all they'd need to know and told them what to expect. So in groups of two they paddled out, and once the waves started forming, he told them to go for it. They all paddled hard and when ready, they jumped up. Most of the kids managed to stay up for what was a long three seconds they all tumbled into the water, getting swallowed into the ocean, just like the young man had done on his first lesson. They all rose from the waves with big smiles on their faces, most of them having mouths full of sea water, while the children on the beach watched and giggled.

They surfed all morning. Some of the kids did well but most spent the morning tumbling into the ocean, not surfing the waves. No matter, they all had smiles on their faces that were radiating joy. Some of the kids actually preferred tumbling into the waves. The young man and the volunteers laughed at these future dare devils in action. They also played games on the beach with the kids before lunch. At lunch, most of the kids were silent to the young man and the other volunteers' surprise; the kids were all transfixed on the ocean, staring at her vast horizon while listening to the waves.

One of the kids, Diego, asked, "Have you really been all the way out there?"

"Yes." the young man replied with a big smile.

CHAPTER 5

Diego's face painted a picture of shocked wonderment. "It must be scary!" he said.

"It can be, but I love it" replied the young man

"I think I love the ocean," Diego said. "I've only seen it once, but I think I love it! I didn't know it was blue."

The young man looked at Diego, saddened. "Have you had a good day?" he asked.

"The best day, now," Diego answered. "Shhhhh, I want to listen to the waves."

The young man smiled at the cheekiness of Diego and nodded in agreement. They spent a few more hours on the beach, but eventually it was time to take them home. All the kids begged, puppy-dog eyes, for a few more minutes to look out to sea. They wanted to take it all in as they didn't know when they would see it again. Eventually they had to go so they all piled on the mini bus again, full of energy, but not for long. The second they sat down they fell asleep!

The drive back wasn't too long. The only one not asleep was Diego; he was sitting at the back looking out of the rear windows, staring at the ocean while the sun set. It broke the young man's heart that there wasn't a lot more he could do for him. When they arrived at the drop-off point, the sliding of the mini bus door woke their sleepy heads and they all got out in a zombie-like state. They were still smiling, though; those smiles hadn't disappeared all day.

Diego was the last one off the bus, the only one not still smiling. The young man stopped him and told him that he could be and do anything he wanted in this world and that he believed in him. He also told Diego that the world loves an underdog, and that he wanted him to go show the world what he's made of.

A little smile appeared on Diego's face and he said, "You really believe in me?"

"Yeah, I really do" the young man answered

Diego just smiled, gave the young man a hug then walked off home, looking back at the young man as he went and before he drifted round the corner he waved.

Raphael asked the young man, "Why did you tell him that?"

The young man replied, "People can do amazing things when someone shows a little belief in them. The worst thing you can do is tell someone they can't do that or you don't believe in them, especially when in a situation such as Diego's. People are capable of unbelievable things and Diego knowing that someone believes he can do whatever he wants may have just changed his life. He already has so many hurdles to jump, there's no need to add anymore. If possible, we should try and take some away."

The next day the young man woke up early, put his coffee in a flask and made his way to the beach. He spent the early morning surfing; the sun had barely risen above the horizon. As the sun rose, he lay there in the ocean, waves gently washing over him, the morning sun now warming his face. He felt as light as a cloud, drifting with the waves, a cool air occasionally brushing over his chest, making a tingling chill as the water dried. All the young man could hear were the waves crashing against the beach and the rocks not so far away. The young man loved Rio's beaches, they captured what he felt a beach should be. Simply, beautiful chaos. A beach is chaotic because it can be unpredictable, change in a blink of an eye. It can drag you out to sea and drown you without a second thought; the waves can crash onto you with almighty force. But is beautiful because it is pure. The sounds of waves, the feeling of sand between your toes and the cold salty water which raises the hairs on your skin, all to be warmed by the glowing warmth of the sun. In its tranquil state, it provides respite from the worries of the mind.

When the young man got out of the sea, his eyes were struck by the most beautiful thing he had ever seen. Smooth cinnamon-tanned skin glowing in the morning sun, wavy golden hair tied up with two strips of hair curled into s's going down her face, gently resting on her cheeks. Her soft lips were angelic; kings of ancient kingdoms would have fought wars for them. Her lips beautifully flowed into her big round cheeks, her jawline was sharp and defined yet smooth and rounded. Her curves were endless, each one flowed to the next. Her emerald green swimsuit complimented her big hazel-green eyes, which were mesmerising and innocent. Everything about this young lady felt like an oasis, a beautiful oasis in the desert of the young man's mind. She couldn't be real – but to his delight, she was.

As he got closer, she looked at him, giving a small but high-cheeked smile. She looked down as though she was embarrassed to hold eye contact for too long, although looking down, she was still beaming with anxious excitement and a little blushing smile.

As the young man got to her, he bent down on one knee and said, "Hi, sorry to disturb you, but I had to come over and tell you I think your absolutely stunning and I just wanted to say hi …"

"Hi, I'm Juliana," she said with an uncontrollable smile which was still beaming with anxious excitement. She told him she was from Rio. They spoke about the carnival, life, their hopes and dreams and pretty much straight away the young man asked whether she had a boyfriend. She said no and the young man's already charming smile grew to a boy-like smile on Christmas day.

Little did they know, but they had been talking for three hours; time had frozen for them, nothing else seemed to matter. They had the waves crashing in the background; it was an orchestra of their itching desire for each other. The young man asked Juliana if she was busy today, and when she said no, the young man asked her if she would like to spend the day with him. She said yes, and so they spent the day exploring the streets of Rio with Juliana showing the young man Rio's hidden gems. They even hiked up to the Christ the Redeemer. The whole day was spent talking and listening to each other. The young man had previously been in relationships, but no one had ever made him feel this way. Juliana told the young man about her ex-boyfriend and said she was scared to get hurt again. But also told him that her biggest desire was to be able to give her heart and soul to someone and for them to give theirs to her. The young man just looked at her and smiled. She looked up at him with a little smile, brushing her hair behind her ear, then put her arm around him.

By the time they got down from the hike, the sun was setting and the young man walked her home. They planned to meet again the next day after she finished work. They eventually arrived at her apartment, walking up some rather steep little steps from the street. As he stood on the doorstep, gave her a kiss on the cheek and said, "Buenas noches" (goodnight in Spanish). They both took one more long gaze at each other, then Juliana slowly closed the door, keeping eye contact with a blushing smile.

The young man slowly strolled down the street, but he missed her already. It had only been about five minutes, but that was five minutes too long! So, he ran back to her doorstep. Knock,

CHAPTER 5

knock, knock. Juliana jumped up, looked through the little eye hole in the door and was surprised to see the young man. She panicked and ran to a mirror to make sure she looked OK.

"Coming!" Juliana opened the door.

The young man said, "I couldn't wait until tomorrow to see you again; would you like to go to dinner?"

"No," she said.

The young man's face painted a picture of heartbreak.

"But you can come in for dinner," she finished.

The young man's boyish smile returned and he said, "Yes, please."

She cooked them both dinner while he sat on a stool and watched. He wandered into the living room and saw it was filled with canvases.

"Did you do all these?" he asked.

Juliana, turning round from a sizzling pan, said, "Yes."

Looking at the artwork the young man replied, "They're great!"

She smiled and said, "Thank you. I try and sell them to galleries and shops. Some get sold, others I just give away to people; if I kept them I wouldn't have any room in my apartment."

Once dinner was ready they went onto the rooftop of her apartment. After dinner, they both lay on the roof, her head and arm resting on his chest, looking at the stars. They wrapped themselves in a tiny blanket, and again spent hours talking under the moonlit sky. Juliana eventually had to go as she had work in the morning. But with this goodbye, they kissed. The young man and Juliana rested their foreheads together, he brushed her hair behind her ear, ran the back of his fingers over her cheek and then gave her one last kiss before he left.

After Juliana closed the door, she rested back on it and let out a hearty breath. A girlish smile appeared; this could be the start of something special. She went over to the window and watched the young man walk off into the night. Once he was out of view, she closed the curtains and fell back on her bed, throwing her hands and feet about in excitement. Ironically, she couldn't sleep that night, and neither could the young man, both of them thinking of one another.

The next day the young man woke up from very little sleep and frantically counted the seconds until he could meet Juliana. He was so eager to see her, that he arrived thirty minutes early at the local restaurant where she was a waitress. He waited across the street on a bench. When Juliana saw him, and a cute little smile appeared on her face.

"What's the smile for?" the owner of the restaurant asked.

"I think the man I'm going to spend the rest of my life with is waiting outside," she said.

"Well, you better go then," the owner replied. "No time to waste when love is involved."

Juliana hung up her apron and walked over to the young man with a beaming smile, radiating joy to anyone who was lucky enough to get a look. She had a little skip in her step and at the last second, ran into his arms. For the young man, the air got a little sweeter, the flowers seemed more colourful, the sun a little brighter. They walked down the street, arm in arm. The young man asked her if she wanted to go sailing. She was excited about this as she had never been sailing before but began to get nervous as she didn't want to get seasick.

They made their way to the marina and the young man welcomed her aboard, giving Juliana a tour of the boat. It only lasted about two minutes because the boat was small. Juliana

CHAPTER 5

laughed at the young man as he was giving the tour like a wildlife documentary.

Then off they went, heading north up the coast. Juliana asked if she could steer the boat and the young man anxiously let her. It went well. Better than well, she was a natural and didn't crash or capsize the boat much to the young man's relief. She didn't feel seasick either. Quite the opposite, actually; she rather enjoyed sailing Delilah.

They set anchor just off the coast. The young mana and Juliana put on some flippers and dived in to explore the enchanting world which lay beneath the sea. They then had their own talent contest to see who could do the best dive from the boat. Juliana won; the young man would tell you he let her win as he was a gentlemen, but the truth is, Juliana won because she was simply better. The young man taught Juliana to spear fish and with a little practice, she caught that night's dinner which would be cooked on the BBQ later. The young man was still trying to figure out Eithan's wife's secret recipe and remained optimistic about it. The afternoon was spent on the boat, talking, and swimming in the sea.

Once they were finished swimming, they lay on the deck of the boat getting some sun. The young man told her about the old man and the night of the bridge. She didn't know what to say, so she curled up closer and tighter to him and said that she was sorry and that she was glad the old man had saved him. The young man smiled and held her tighter. Although it had only been two days, it was as though they had known each other for years; it was almost like destiny had allowed their souls to collide. As they lay on the deck, both of them wanted to say 'I love you', but neither did – they didn't want to scare the other away. But why should you have to wait to scream to the heavens a declaration of love? Why should you have to fear the power an 'I love you' holds?

As the day drew on, the young man told Juliana about his tradition of watching the sunset and stargazing in the night sky. He told her about the old man and the three legged chair. She loved it and the young man, but she was scared to tell him.

"I could get used to this," she said. The young man just smiled, looking into her eyes. He didn't say anything, as all he wanted to say was 'I love you, and I want to travel the world with you' but he was worried she would say no and he wanted this moment to last forever.

The young man walked inside the cabin and began playing some music; he opened the windows so it could escape and float around the deck. He started playing the disc and began banging his head in time with the music. As he walked out onto the deck, he began playing air guitar, letting the music take him away. Juliana watched him, laughing but in the good kind of way. A small rogue wave knocked the young man off balance mid song, and he tumbled down onto the deck. While on all fours, he gave Juliana a quick kiss, took her hand and pulled her up and they both began playing air guitar, moving round the deck of the boat to the beat of the music. Song after song they rocked it out, having their own party on the deck off the Brazilian coast. They finished their air guitar and jamming session by running and jumping off the side of the boat, arms in the air with rock star gestures as they plunged into the water. A cannon ball was the entry method of choice, bigger splash, all the others just didn't fit the moment. In the sea, they treaded water. Juliana wrapped her arms round the young man's neck and they kissed, music still escaping from the windows. In the young man's mind he liked to think the waves were rocking with them. A little crazy,

CHAPTER 5

but he though a little crazy kept you sane and made things a bit more fun. They now moved to the end of the boat and sat with their feet dipped in the water, towels wrapped round their necks. The boat was lit up by fairy lights; the young man had spent the morning putting them up.

Juliana asked the young man, "How long are you staying in Rio for?"

The young man replied, "I was going to leave today, but I think I'm going to stay a while now."

Juliana grinned and cheekily said, "Because of me?"

The young man smiled, ad looked into her eyes and said, "Yes, because of you."

They finished watching the sunset which was a perfect way to end their day together and a perfect way to start the night together. They then spent the remainder of the evening going through the old man's awesome collection of vinyl; he had boxes filled with classics. The corners of the covers were a little worn, which were like little love scars. They belted out these classics well into the night and were singing to their hearts' content.

In the early morning, the young man sailed the boat back along the Brazilian coastline into the marina, with a sun that had barley risen above the horizon. Juliana was in the cabin, asleep, wrapped up in the same blanket the old man had given him on the night of the bridge. She laid there, so innocent, and the young man loved the little snore she did when she was in a deep sleep; it was a mixture of a baby piglet and an angry truck driver tooting his horn. They had spent the night stargazing and the young man told Juliana about where he was planning to travel. She had never travelled before and her eyes lit up with excitement as the young man told her about the places he was going and where he had been. He showed her his map with the route he had so carefully planned, as well as the pictures of his journey so far. The young man still had the napkin he had first drawn his map on at Isabella's café; this was second favourite for Juliana, second only to a picture of him and Eithan.

As they pulled up to the marina, the young man tied the boat up and then tiptoed across the deck, trying not to make a sound. He leaned into the cabin, and in a soft voice, said, "Juliana ... Juliana."

She didn't wake up so he called her again and she sleepily woke, with one eye closed, and smiled at the sight of him. She yawned and had a wide morning kind of stretch. They hugged with a true desire for time to freeze; in that moment all they wanted to do was live a thousand lives in the eyes of one another. Juliana had to leave. She wore the young man's lucky hoodie. She smelled the inside of the hoodie as she walked out the marina as she missed the young man already; the smell of his hoodie would have to be enough until they saw each other again.

A week had a passed. The young man and Juliana had spent almost every day together; they grew closer by the second, and with every second spent together, every second apart felt like a lifetime.

The young man had no plans with Juliana until the evening. So he went hiking and spent most of the time talking to himself. Muttering words over and over again, trying different combinations, some of them being rubbish, he was rehearsing a question he had for Juliana, but he couldn't seem to find the right words. He wanted to ask her to come with him; he wanted her to sail the world with him and live like renegades, the sea air in their face and freedom on the horizon, each day a new adventure. He wanted to ask her but he wanted the right words;

CHAPTER 5

he couldn't find them. With each step he took, his mind raced. The Brazilian sun beat down on him, almost as a punishment for not knowing the words. Then the heavens opened, and it rained on a Biblical scale. The young man sat on a rock looking over the bay of Rio. He thought of how far he had come from where he was on that night of the bridge. When he closed his eyes, he was back there. He could remember every detail: the pouring rain, the cold emptiness of the night that mirrored the feeling in his soul. He could hear the rain droplets ricocheting off the metal beams on the bridge. He could remember the feeling of his hands and mind slowly loosening their grip on the railing. He could remember falling, and the impact of colliding with the water. As his mind remembered this, he woke from the daydream and looked up at the sky with the rain pouring over him. He smiled as he now thought of what the future held, and he had hope. The young man didn't worry about the words for Juliana anymore, he knew he would have them when the time came.

He started walking down a rocky part of the coast and saw some locals diving into the sea. It was still raining, and the young man had only swam in the rain once, but he thought there was nothing like it: the freeing feeling it gave him, the sounds of the rain colliding with the water, the view from under the water. So, the young man spent a little time with some locals diving into the water. Some of the locals offered the young man one a go on a paddleboard, and they didn't have to ask him twice. They paddled out to sea a little, forming a circle all sitting on their boards and started splashing with the paddles.

It's good to play like children sometimes," said of the locals. "It keeps the mind and soul young and alive." The young man sat on his board with the rain coming down on him, the water droplets now rolling down his face and dripping off his chin like a leaky pipe.

The young man and Juliana had planned to meet at a restaurant. It was in an old colonial building which was a faded baby blue and orange with the white of the building exposed underneath. It had a large grand white doorway and a wooden sign above the door that read 'Sofia's'. The young man waited for Juliana to arrive. He had bought a new shirt for dinner – a black linen shirt – which he wore with a few buttons undone. The young man would later tell Juliana it was because of the heat, but really he just wanted to show Juliana he was a man because he had a few hairs on his chest! The evening heat made his tanned cheeks a little red; the streetlamps made the path turn orange. And then she arrived – Juliana in a red silk dress. The young man was absolutely speechless; he had never seen anything or anyone as beautiful. He grinned and slowly began to walk towards her. She grinned at him.

He took her by her hands and said, "I'm speechless ... you look stunning, absolutely gorgeous."

Juliana cheekily said, "You don't look too bad yourself."

They went in, talked, looked into each other's eyes the whole evening and ate some of the best food they had ever had. After dinner, they walked back to the young man's boat and sat on the wooden deck.

As they lay beneath the stars, the young man said, "Juliana, do you want to travel the world with me? I know you probably think I'm crazy and we haven't known each other that long but I love you, and I want to see the word with you and ..."

Juliana interrupted. "Stop talking. Yes, I thought you were never going to ask."

The young man smiled and then Juliana said, "Oh, and I love

CHAPTER 5

you too." She kissed him and then looked up at the stars. They both lay there smiling, looking into the expanse of the universe and dreamed of future days gone by.

Later on in the evening, he asked Juliana if she would miss her friends.

"It's hard to make friends in this modern world. Everything's online; it's supposed to make us more connected but it makes me feel more alone. Plus I like being at home doing my art anyway, I'm a lot more comfortable in my dungarees with my music keeping me company."

The young man looked at Juliana and said, "I hope you know you have a boyfriend and friend now and I have an opening for a position of best friend if you would like it."

Juliana laughed and gave a scrunched-up kind of smile, then said, "Hmmm let me think about that, I think I would like that but is there a return policy?"

They both laughed and before the young man could say a word, she kissed him.

Chapter 6

The young man and Juliana spent another week together in Rio; Juliana had a few things to take care of before they went off on their travels. In that week they also continued to explore the city together and the young man even organised another day out with the kids from the favelas. Juliana came this time and the kids loved her; it seemed everywhere she went people just fell in love with her. The kids were just as excited as last time and still loved tumbling into the sea more than riding the waves. The night before they were going to leave the young man cooked dinner and laid a table on the deck of Delilah; it was a dinner to celebrate the adventure they were about to embark upon.

The day of departure soon arrived; Juliana anxiously got aboard with her last bag of things. They set sail, with Rio gradually becoming smaller and smaller. Juliana now felt the freedom, the same freedom the young man had felt when he first left. They had freedom brushing through their hair, adventure on the horizon and love in their hearts.

The young man and Juliana had been at sea now for two days and they'd loved every second of it. She wasn't a bad sailor and the young man wasn't a bad teacher. They followed the coastline and stopped when Juliana found something to explore.

CHAPTER 6

They were heading for the beautiful city of Buenos Aires in Argentina and were four days' sailing away.

On the fourth day of sailing, as they neared their destination, they came across three humpback whales. The young man looked at Juliana and said, "Want to jump in?" So, flippers and goggles on, they plunged into the freezing water of the South Atlantic and swam with the giant creatures. They got so close they could touch them, both awestruck at what they were doing. Never in his wildest dreams would the young man have ever thought he would be swimming with whales, travelling the world with a woman who he loved. Treading water, listening to the waves, looking at the whales and Juliana, the young man smiled. He had moments of nirvana and in those moments everything was blissful. This was soon broken and became laughter as Juliana was splashed by one of the whales as it came up above the water and dived back down

The young man dived under, using his flippers to aid him, and Juliana soon followed. They floated in the aquatic world and swam next to the whales, the whales twisting and turning as they glided through the water They managed to swim within metres of the whales and for the few minutes they could hold their breath, they felt like they were in another world. They re-emerged from the ocean's depths for air, to then dive back down to swim with these majestic creatures again. On the second dive down the young man was facing one of the whales as it rose to the surface for air and the young man saw one of the whales breach the water from under the oceans depths and then crash back down. The bubbles in the water were like confetti to the whale's spectacular performance.

As they arrived in the port it was pouring down with rain. They tied the boat up and hid in the cabin, hoping the rain would stop. When it didn't they decided to run and dance in the rain; street by street they embraced the new city and the downpour. The day was spent exploring the city in the rain seeing the remains of the Spanish colonial rule and grand cathedrals. The young man and Juliana went into local cafes and shops, and wandered the streets and got lost. The young man loved getting lost in new cities and Juliana was just in love with travel; this was her first time out of Brazil.

The rain only made the city seem more vibrant, more alive. If the city was a flower, the rain made it blossom. On their exploration they came across the city's opera house. Juliana had always wanted to go to the opera and looked at the young man with big puppy-dog eyes and said, "Do you want to go?"

The young man smiled and said, "Yes."

In excitement, Juliana started singing in the rain; the young man joined in her spontaneous display of joy. They started splashing in the puddles that lined the path around the opera house. The rainfall soaked them to the bone; they soon got cold so walked back to the boat and dried off in the cabin, rubbing their hair with towels, leaving them with frizzy damp hair. The young man and Juliana lay on the bed listening to music from the old man's vinyl player. They would play rock paper scissors when the needle ran off the record and whoever lost the intense game, had to put the next record on.

A day had passed already, and the young man had got Juliana a hotel room for the day; they were going to the opera tonight and they wanted to get ready separately so they could meet up later in the hotel bar. Juliana thought it would add suspense and a thrill to the evening.

The young man bought a tuxedo and spent the late morning and early afternoon in the tailor's shop. It took a while to fit the

CHAPTER 6

suit for the young man, but he didn't mind; he told the tailor all about Juliana. The tailor was a good listener and a sucker for young love. The young man stood in front of a set of mirrors with the tailor taking his measurements and pinning the jacket into position. They had their conversation via the mirror as the tailor was strict and told the young man to not move too much.

The tailor said, "You love this girl?"

The young man replied, "Yes, madly."

The tailor then said, "Make sure she knows that every day. In thirty years of marriage, I haven't gone a day without telling my wife I love her."

The young man smiled into the mirror at the tailor and gave him a nod. " Yes, sir," he said. "I bet you have some good stories; you have probably met more people in your lifetime than most."

The tailor, with a smile and a look of reminiscence, said, "Yes, I've got a story or two ... but I want to hear more about this lady, Juliana, and your travels."

So they continued talking; the young man told him more about his travels and spoke about missing Eithan. The young man was persistent, however, and the tailor quickly realised this; he wanted to hear one of the tailor's stories and he eventually gave into the young man's charm and persistence.

The tailor said, "I was tailoring a suit for a big politician who had paid me more money for discretion. As the morning proceeded, the politician began talking to his colleagues who were also being measured for suits. They spoke about things I just couldn't unhear; they made me boil with moral rage. As I fitted their suits for them, I entered a moral dilemma: on one hand, I would break a moral code if I went against the silence I had sworn to but, on the other hand, my morals were being tested by the politician and his colleagues. I spent the whole morning going over it in my mind. I am a man of my word but on that occasion, I couldn't be. I had to speak out. So, I went to the papers and I told people at the bar and used my voice to fight my moral outrage. By doing so, I sparked a mini revolutionary protest, which by the end had done more good than bad. The politicians were arrested, and the people had risen up and fought for the beliefs they held dear."

That might not have been the most interesting or well told story, but there's something in it I think.

The young man said, "What's that?"

The tailor continued. "Never underestimate the power of your voice and the power of words. Words can build nations and movements, but they can also crumble them. Words hold a power that are incomparable."

The young man then said, "I never thought about it that way before, that's great!"

The tailor shook his head and said, "No, not great, just powerful. Power can be good and bad so we must be careful with the words we say and the words we allow into our minds."

Later, the young man arrived at the hotel and waited for Juliana at the bar. He sat on a bar stool, one foot on the ground, one foot on the stool. He adjusted his bow tie and cuffs then took a sip of his drink. He turned his head to the bar entrance and their she was – cinnamon ecstasy wrapped up in a seductively elegant black dress. He was speechless. As he stood up, he looked her up and down. Juliana, being shy at the young man's look of lust, looked down and brushed her hair behind her ear with a little smile. The young man walked over, slowly lifted her head by her chin and kissed her. The kiss forced her to her tiptoes as she didn't want it to end; she was in another world, a world where this kiss would never end. The young man got the receptionist to call them a taxi; while they waited for it to arrive, they sat at the bar.

The taxi took them straight to the opera house; it wasn't far, only a five minute drive. The streetlights whizzed past, all blurring into one through the window. They arrived and the young man quickly ran round to Juliana's door to open it; tonight was going to be a night of undying chivalry. They walked across the street arm in arm, both gazing up at the beautiful opera house. It came alive that night. The light spilled through the windows towards the queues of eager opera goers all dressed up for the night's performance. The young man and Juliana were full of excitement of the unknown the night would bring.

Once they got into the opera house, they sat in the lounge waiting for the show to begin. About fifteen minutes had passed when a call came over a speaker system telling them that the show was about to begin. After the announcement everyone made their way to their seats.

The stage was encompassed by an array of seating. The ceiling must have been over twenty metres tall, with a stunning chandelier lighting the room surrounded by beautiful artwork. The young man and Juliana sat engrossed; each performance, each note, each song was powerful and energized their souls. At the bar they had got talking to the bar tender.

"Your first time?" he asked them

"Yes," said Juliana

"Well, you'll either love it and forever be changed, or not, and just have a nice evening," the bar tender said.

The young man and Juliana loved it and would forever be changed. Moments of the performance had the hairs on their bodies raised. The first half of the performance had come to an end and they couldn't believe it as it seemed a matter of minutes ago it had begun. But the curtain drew and the lights came on; the interval had commenced.

During the interval, the young man went to the bar and while he was away, a slightly older lady tapped Juliana on the shoulder. They began talking about the performance and she told Juliana she thought they were a cute couple. She added that she thought the young man was very handsome. The lady had had a few drinks so was quite forthcoming to Juliana, maybe a little too much. The lady's friend apologised in case she had offended Juliana and the friends began bickering, the friendly kind. Juliana faced the front and giggled to herself.

When the young man arrived back from the bar, he was welcomed with a beaming smile from Juliana. She told the young man what had just happened and how she had to hold back the laughter.

When he laughed, Juliana said, "Don't laugh, they will know we're talking about them."

"You might have some competition now," he joked.

Juliana frowned and lightly punched the young man on his arm. "I'm only joking," he said. "There's no competition with you in the picture." Her frown quickly became a smile.

The lights slowly dimmed, drawing everyone's attention to the stage, the curtain rose, and the performance began again. The young man took Juliana's hand, interlocking their fingers. Juliana, squeezing the young man's hand, looked at him, smiling, while biting her lip. The young man didn't think the performance could get any better but was he wrong; the song that ended the night's performance played the strings of his heart and soul. It would be stored in his psyche for eternity. The curtain pulled across the stage and the lights slowly began to illuminate the room. The young man and Juliana sat there for a moment, taking in what they had just experienced. They slowly followed the crowd back out into the lounge. They saw the bartender through the crowds and the young man smiled and put his hand over his heart then gave him a nod of acknowledgment. The bartender knew they had fallen in love with the performance and he gave a nod to them.

They strolled outside and the young man put his jacket over Juliana's shoulders. Taxis lined the street outside the opera house, the young man and Juliana walked over quickly as they didn't want the taxis to get pouched by other operagoers. They hurried into one and told the driver where they wanted to go – this time to a restaurant that the young man's tailor had recommended. The taxi dropped them off down a wobbly cobbled street lit by warm yellow streetlights.

As the young man and Juliana opened the door, they closed it again swiftly because of the small chance that any of the energy in the room they had just been struck by could escape; it was a risk too high. Their bodies shivered in the warmth, shaking off the cool air. The atmosphere filled the small room; everyone was smiling and merry. The food was plentiful, and the drink flowed like the Nile; you received a service of royal standards. The waiters were all suited, wearing dress gloves; career servers of this kind are a dying breed, so the young man and Juliana experienced the suave and urbane service while they still could. All the tables were close together. Sitting at the tables, they could hear the bartenders mixing drinks with the sounds of scratchy clinking of the ice. It was nice. Although you were having a private intimate dinner, everything about the restaurant made you feel like one living organism; you were all on this dining journey together, all in harmony with one another, all beating to the same rhythm and adding to this little slice of utopia.

The couple next to the young man and Juliana told them to order the wife's special; the restaurant was owned by a husband and wife. The wife was the head chef and every night she made a new special. She would go to the market every morning to pick the ingredients for the new menu. It was food Russian roulette but if each empty chamber were an explosive delight and then the chamber that had a bullet in was a culinary marvel, the kind of dish where the chef would have sold their soul to the devil for, and the kind of dish that made locals and travellers alike keep coming back.

The waiters never let a glass become empty – full glass, full heart, the waiters said. The young man and Juliana had never drank so much in their lives, but they had never eaten so much either, so it balanced itself out. Well, kind of. The restaurant gave smaller portions but a lot of dishes! Plate after plate came, each one getting seemingly better than the last, each bite melting the taste buds to euphoria. When you weren't eating your mouth watered at the thought of what was to come. They ordered the wife's special, after the couple next to them recommended it and a bottle of something local to share with the couple next to them. As they sat there, drinking with their now second bottle of something local, they caught a glimpse of the next couple who entered the restaurant. They could see that the couple were also struck by the atmosphere and they too closed the door swiftly, afraid to let the essence of this establishment escape.

After they had finished their second bottle of something local with the couple next to them, they said goodnight and they tipped their waiter generously; the service they received

CHAPTER 6

deserved nothing less. As they left, they took one more look into the restaurant, all their five senses firing on all cylinders. They gave a farewell wave to the waiter and to the couple they had shared more than a drink or two with. As they opened the door, they were tickled by a cool chilling breeze that ran over their bodies. They closed the door behind them, entering the moonlit streets of Buenos Aires. On their way home they walked arm in arm, Juliana wearing the young man's jacket, the collar up as if she thought she was a rockstar. They slowly made their way back to the boat and once they arrived, they fell asleep with merry minds, souls, and bodies, curled up to each other in the clouds of their bed.

The young man woke up in his shirt and trousers, bow tie and jacket surprisingly placed neatly over a chair. He made his way to the kitchen which was only about four metres away from the bed but might as well have been four miles for the young man's head. He began making some coffee and the smell blew through the cabin, waking Juliana. She lay on the bed, half under the covers, peeking out every so often to check on the progress of the coffee, but quickly going back under as the morning was a little too bright for her, so under the covers she laid waiting. The young man arrived with a cup of revitalisation which was undoubtingly needed. They drank their coffee in bed with the warmth of the covers and the chill that came from the morning air. The cabin door creaked as the wind gently rocked it back and forth.

They spent the late morning exploring more of the city and in the late afternoon, with a sudden burst of rain drenching them, they ran for cover, hiding under a little ledge that provided safety from the downpour.

Then they ran again, hoping to find refuge from the rain.

They went down a little street and came across a bar called El Sonrisa, which translates into 'the sunrise'. As they entered, they were immersed into this seductive dimly lit ballroom bar, with elegantly masculine music playing. In the centre were couples dancing, arm in arm, eyes locked on each other. The couples were passionately strutting around the dance floor in perfect time, each step made the floor rumble, you could feel it ripple up your leg. The raw power of the dance was intoxicating. The young man and Juliana ordered some drinks and sat at a table, watching the story unfold. The dance was unique for all those lucky enough to witness it –the Argentinian tango evokes different emotions, pulling on the cords of the heart in different ways. For the young man it was a story of lovers who had one last night together. He imagined that the man was off to war and this would be their last dance for what would feel like eternity. They were laying their hearts out on the dance floor, both dancers living and breathing what they were feeling – each breath, each step saying a thousand words. The young man saw what would be left of love if you stripped it back; he saw two people, one soul, their hearts and bodies entwined, a connection so strong an army couldn't tear them apart, their display of love and passion laid their heart on the dance floor for all to see. It was an autopsy of love. On stage, a small band were playing the instruments to within an inch of their lives. They all wore midnight purple shirts and black hats with feathers in them. Each member of the band was wearing a different coloured feather. Behind them, illuminating the stage, was a red neon sign which read El Sonrisa. The brick walls, burgundy leather seats, walnut wooden tables and even the bartenders all wearing a jet black uniform, all came together to create an intense environment that added to the passion in each footstep, each turn, each kick, each lift of the dancers' feet. The intensity in the room was only cooled down for a brief moment when you sipped your drink, but then you were pulled straight back into the passion-fuelled inferno.

The young man and Juliana sat there, mesmerised by the beauty and power of the women as they strutted around the men with purpose and potency. The men had their shoulders back and chest up, with a red-blooded confidence that controlled the dance floor. The raw masculinity and luscious femininity of the dancers transcended everyone in the room into a realm of unknown emotion. Both the young man and Juliana had fallen in love with the alluring and seductive Argentinian tango. They looked into each other's eyes, the gatekeepers to the soul, and once unlocked they saw the deepest and darkest depths of each other like never before. Neither smiled. No, this was not the place for smiling. The passionate exploration through each other's eyes into one another's souls demanded a smouldering intensity. A smile would have broken this.

An older couple, Santiago, and Isabella were their names, came up to the young man and Juliana and asked if they would like to dance. Without hesitation, they said, yes. The older man took Juliana's hand and the older woman took the young man's hand and they guided them into the sea of dancers. The older couple directed their new partner in the art of the Argentinian tango; each step, each turn, each kick, each lift they got a little better.

Soon the older lady said, "You're ready to lead your lady. Now go, shoulders back, chest up, and dance as one."

The young man took hold of Juliana; her body fit perfectly into his hands and they danced. They danced, holding each other all through the night into the early hours of the morning.

With each step, they added to the rumble of floor which the band seemed to effortlessly be in harmony with. Each step they took added to the intensity in the room, sweat now dripping down their faces, with the warm lights which lit the dance floor ever so slightly now seeming to only be shining on them. It was as if they were the only ones in the room. No, the only ones in the world.

Santiago and Isabella looked at the young couple and he said, "They're naturals!"

"No, my love, they are just one ... they are just one soul," Isabella replied.

The morning sun started peering through the cracks in the door and windows. The sunlight became a silent alarm awakening everyone from a trance-like state the dance and El Sonrisa had put them in.

The older couple tapped them on the shoulder and said, "Come with us."

So the young man and Juliana walked with them. They went onto the roof of the bar and the older gentleman told them why the bar was called El Sonrisa. "This place makes you dance into the morning sun." Both couples stood on the roof and watched the sunrise.

"This is the real Argentina, rising by the sun and dancing by the moon," the older woman said.

A few moments passed and the older man said, "So do you like our bar?"

The young man and Juliana smiled at each other. "We love it!" they said.

"Good," said the older man. "So, we will see you again later?"

"Later? You guys do this every night?"

Santiago looked stunned that the young man would even ask

that. He said, "We do it whenever we want and however long we want to. Some weeks we dance every night!"

"Yes, we will definitely come later," said Juliana, "but we need a little sleep first."

As the young man and Juliana walked down the street, they found a café, ordered breakfast and watched the world go by. The streets slowly came alive and soon they could hear the hustling sounds of the city bouncing off the colonial-style buildings.

After breakfast, they slowly walked back to the boat and slept the rest of the morning and part of the early afternoon – they needed a little sleep before tonight! Afterwards, they ventured out onto the streets once again on their way to meet the older couple at their bar. As they arrived, Santiago, Isabella and their staff were putting out the chairs, checking stock and polishing tables for the night ahead. They saw the young man and Juliana walk in and smiled, welcoming them with hugs. They sat down at a freshly polished table and talked about how they had met, their journey so far, and the young man told them of his journey too. Santiago and Isabella told them about how they had met as kids and that they had loved each other faithfully for thirty years.

"We'll let you know a little secret on how we have stayed together this long and most of the time loved each other like we did as teenagers," Isabella said.

Both the young man and Juliana awaited her wisdom, intrigued by what she was going to say. They were both hungry for the not-so-secret recipe to a long passionate relationship.

"We've kept it spontaneous and exciting, we talk and never sleep on an argument. These two little things have made us fall in love each day. You need to grow as individuals and also grow as a team."

The older couple then gave the young man and Juliana a dancing lesson. The band was there rehearsing for the night ahead and the bar staff were prepping the bar. They danced around the staff to the sounds of the band's near perfect rehearsal. During the lesson, the young man and Juliana followed Santiago and Isabella's lead; they all strutted around the empty dance floor, learning new steps and perfecting their tango. When they took little breaks, the young man and Juliana helped prep the bar.

After the lesson, the young man and Juliana went up to the roof with a bottle of tequila and a couple of glasses. They watched the sunset and started talking; their conversations would always drift and go off into unknown destinations. They loved talking about big topics and asked unanswerable questions, the kind that leave you puzzled and curious.

Then the night had arrived, and they danced. They danced until the morning sun. When the sun rose, and the dancing was over, the young man and Juliana sat on the steps outside the bar as the sunlight began to peer over the buildings and warm their faces, the shadows retreating with every passing minute.

They heard the swinging of the door – it was Santiago. He came out and stood just below the steps, enjoying the moment with them. A few moments later, he invited the young couple to the family ranch just outside the city. He told them that every other weekend the family met there, and he would love them to meet everyone before they left. He said it would only be for a couple of days. Juliana looked at the young man and then looked at Santiago. She said, "We would love to." As he walked back in, he turned back and looked at the young couple for a second, and he reminisced on old memories with Isabella. The

CHAPTER 6

young man and Juliana reminded him of himself and Isabella.

The young man and Juliana patiently waited on the steps of the bar for Santiago and Isabella, their weekend bags packed. . A car soon pulled up with the two loved up oldies in. Santiago piled the bags in and they set off driving through the city's stunning streets together. Santiago had a classic car which the young man adored, and once they were out of the city, Santiago let the young man drive the rest of the way to the ranch.

The ranch was stunning. They pulled up to the drive and the entrance had a big wooden arch with a sign saying, 'Amarilla Hierro Rancho'. Isabella told them that it translated to English as 'yellow iron ranch'. She said that had her great grandad named it that because yellow flowers grow over the land here and in her great grandad's words 'you need an iron will to be an Argentinian farmer'. The driveway was long and winding and eventually they pulled up to the main house which sat surrounded by hills. They got out of the car and took in this beautifully designed house. Santiago told them it was made of local wood. The black tiled roof was radiating heat. Isabella said the house was built by her great grandad and his brother and had been passed down to all the family from generation to generation. They walked into a courtyard filled with the most beautiful arrangement of flowers and scrubs, all pruned and maintained to look like artwork. They were the pride and joy of Santiago's and Isabella's daughter; Santiago said she was the best florist in all of Argentina.

The young man and Juliana entered the house where some of the family were waiting for them. They all greeted each other and embraced each other like they had just returned from war. Isabella's sister gave the grand tour; she was a performer and rather outgoing, so she was the right person for the job. The family had welcomed the young man and Juliana to their family home as if they were long lost family members.

A little later the rest of the family arrived. The young man and Juliana had a little giggle together, joking that there were truckloads of family coming. They both came from relatively small families, so it was a shock to them both to see so many people in one house. Everyone gathered around a huge table overlooking the vast hilly landscape of the ranch.

The young man wasn't religious, and neither was Juliana, although she was raised Christian. The family all took each other's hands, closed their eyes and bowed their heads while Santiago, at the head of the table, said grace. He blessed the family, the food, and their guests. They ate the most delicious food; everyone had brought their own dishes to the ranch and laid them on the table.

The night was lit by candles that lined the centre of the table, the wax on the candles dripping down like melting ice cream and drying quickly before it could reach the bottom. The flames danced in the breeze, while complementing the warmth the family were already giving off. The young man and Juliana felt at home; the feeling of family was like a warm fire on a winter's night. They all sat around the table telling each other stories of what had been going on in their lives the past month. They shared a few drinks and some laughter, just spending time with loved ones and escaping the routines of their daily lives. The young man noticed how happy Santiago was. He sat back and watched everyone talking and smiling, the kids running around playing, and for a moment he didn't talk to anyone, he was just looking around at his family, admiring each and every one of them. Santiago was a passionate and emotional man and his eyes told a story of a man who had found his happiness.

CHAPTER 6

The young man smiled at Santiago and he gave him a nod and a smile back. The young man took Juliana's hand and held it tight, using his thumb to feel all the lines in her palm and her fingertips. Juliana looked at him and smiled. The young man thought to himself, He may have found his happiness, but being with Juliana and travelling the world with her makes me happy.

Once everyone started going off to bed, Isabella showed the young man and Juliana to their room and once inside and laid on the bed, they fell asleep straight away. When they woke up and opened the curtains, he smiled and dragged Juliana over so she could see; it was beautiful, just rolling hills.

The young man said, "Now that you're up, do you want to go for a walk?" Out they went into the rolling hills, the wind brushing against the grass and the sun bouncing off the hillsides. "Santiago says that walks in nature are good for the mind; he starts every day in nature," commented the young man.

After they had finished their walk and had some breakfast at the house, Santiago and his son took the young man and Juliana on a tour around the ranch on horseback Neither one of them had been on a horse before but once they were on and riding, they loved it. They followed the trails in the ranch for parts of the tour then went off the beaten track to the grassy hills for other parts of the tour. They had been on horseback for about an hour, when they reached 'the spot'. The spot was one of the highest points of the ranch from where they overlooked the yellow flower fields and down on the house. The sea was in view in the distance. They all sat on their horses in silence and just looked; moments like this required silence, words wouldn't do the moment justice. After this they made their way back to the house and had some breakfast at the table with the family.

The young man and Juliana spent the whole weekend with the family; they played games in the evenings and spent the days exploring the land, playing with the kids and having conversations. But when Sunday came, they all had to go back to their routines and day-to-day lives until they all met back at the ranch in two weeks' time. The drive back was bitter sweet; everyone in the car was dosed up on happiness from the weekend, but there were under tones of sadness as they knew this was the end of their time together and a goodbye was imminent. The drive back was just a beautiful as it was on the way there, if not more so as the young man and Juliana knew they were leaving today so they saw it in more detail; it was like their eyes finally saw the landscape for it's real beauty.

The young man and Juliana were dropped off at the marina. They all took their time to get out of the car; they wanted a few more minutes in each other's company but eventually they had to say goodbye to their new friends. Santiago, with his arm around Isabella, left them with a piece of farewell advice.

"For a willing heart, life is but a beautiful journey."

The young man muttered the words 'for a willing heart, life is but a journey' and smiled; repeating his words allowed them to take true affect. Santiago, now arm in arm with Isabella, looked at the young man and Juliana, and with a father-like smile, said, "You can have and do anything you want; you just have to be willing to struggle for it. Struggle is the essence of our humanity." Then they all hugged, holding on for a few more seconds, their grip getting tighter as the hug was coming to an end. After the hugs they parted ways, walking off, waving farewell as they walked out of sight.

Chapter 7

The young man stood at the helm of the boat envisioning what it must have been like to have to be an old explorer, the kind who gallantly went where no one had been before. The kind who didn't have the internet to check the place first; they were pioneers with just a compass and a brave heart. These explorers didn't know what they were going to find, they just set sail with a yearning and desire to explore, continuing a grand tradition we humans all share, pushing boundaries and finding answers to questions we didn't know to ask ...

He stood there wrapped up in layers of jumpers, with an oatmeal coloured beanie which the young man called Shackleton, after the explorer. Wearing the beanie was like wearing an adventure. Every time the young man wore his Shackleton beanie Juliana would try and put on an English accent and say, "Where we of to now, captain?" This would always bring a smile to the young man's face and make him laugh. Her accent was awful and sometimes she would drink from a cup with her pinkie pointed, just for extra effect.

Juliana adjusted the young man's Shackleton beanie to cover his ears before she sat down and wrapped herself up in blankets, she sat sketching the young man and Delilah; she liked using sticks of charcoal which made her fingers turn black, little layer of charcoal laid in the deck when she blew the little fragments which rested on the page...

They were heading for Chile. The young man and Juliana had planned to hike and climb in the Patagonian mountain ranges. Since she was a little girl, Juliana had wanted to come here.

The mountain ranges looked like they were forged by giants; something this beautiful couldn't be just a by-product of nature. The young man and Juliana looked on in amazement as they sailed on by. They started making up a story together; one would give a line then the other would follow, envisioning their story with a childlike imagination.

The young man said, "Giants use to roam the earth many years ago."

Juliana then followed with, "They split off into groups in search of the most beautiful place on earth."

"One group came across the Patagonia Mountains," he then said.

"They carried giant tools with them," she continued.

"So they could have a giant throne to look upon their most beautiful place on earth ..."

The giant ice fields made the young man's boat look tiny. He thought they were some of nature's grand architecture. He thought each crack was hand crafted by mother nature herself. The water they were sailing through was semi-frozen and the boat broke the thin layer of ice as it journeyed forwards. As they continued on, a piece of the ice field broke off and they could hear the crackles in the air; birds which were on a little ice island flew off with a big flutter. Then, with a mighty Goliath-like roar, the ice broke off and crashed into the sea, creating a spectacle the like of which they had not seen since seeing the humpback whales. As they watched in excitement, they immediately prepared themselves for the boat to be rocked by the large waves now heading for them. It started rocking heavily; inside the cabin plates tumbled onto the floor and the sails started swinging with force (but the ropes kept them tamed) as the waves tried to set them free. Both Juliana and the young man stood there with adrenaline-fuelled laughter. For a second the young man thought the boat might tip over but, thankfully, they had just experienced one of nature's very own roller coasters.

Once the waves had settled down and the boat had stopped rocking, they could now see an island which soon became occupied by birds. It was most likely a safe haven from their evil nemeses ... seals. The young man and Juliana had seen a seal get a bird from one of these islands; the seal sneaked up stealthily and when the moment was right, it leaped and took hold of the bird. Juliana covered her face and hit the young man lightly on the shoulder saying, "Make it stop." The young man giggled, but only a little, and said, "You want me to go and wrestle a seal to stop it?"

"Nooo," she replied in a childlike voice and, with a frowning smile, hit him on the arm again for laughing at her. On their journey together they had witnessed both the beauty and the horror of nature, but like Eithan had taught the young man, without the bad there is no good and without the good there is no bad.

They had sailed through the icy waters of the South Atlantic following the rocky coastline of Argentina and Chile. They arrived in a small marina that rested on the side of the Chilean fjords. It wasn't very big, enough for about half a dozen boats, although that didn't matter as they were the only ones there.

The air was brisk and little clouds formed with each breath. They left the boat and walked along a wooden path that followed the water line; the water was so clear and undisturbed that a perfect reflection of the sharp mountains mirrored off the water. The young man kicked a little stone into the lake. It skimmed along the surface and sent out ripples that blurred the reflection of the mountains. The young man loved how small the mountains and the ice fields made him feel, and how insignificant they made him feel. It strangely comforted him; it set him free, knowing his life was his. The young man looked at them and thought about how they had been there for millions of years and would continue to be there for over a million more years to come; he was but a spec of time in this mountain's life.

They spent the day walking in the grassy hills and hiking up the mountainous landscape. After a good few hours they were high enough to get a good view; they spun around and had views of Patagonia everywhere they looked. The young man and Juliana were going to camp under the stars tonight, so they kept hiking to find the perfect spot to make camp. They wandered the grassy paths which had been stomped out by travellers gone by

Once they had set up camp, the young man looked at Juliana and said, "Want to jump in?" They had set up camp next to the piercing blue lake that sat at the base of the mountains and the sun was beginning to set. They had a fire burning ready for their hasty retreat from the lake. They arrived at the water's edge, both down to their underwear. The young man turned to Juliana and before he could get any words out, she pushed him in. He gasped for air; he wasn't ready for the chilling cold he was now experiencing. He shot up, wiping the water from his face, brushing his hair back while also straining it. He looked

CHAPTER 7

at Juliana and said, "You!" while laughing. He then picked up Juliana in his arms, walked into the lake, wading through the water until it was just below his hips. He looked at her, gave her a kiss, and smiled. He then said, "You ready?" with a cheeky laugh. Then he threw her in the icy waters of the lake. She gasped for air and seconds later, started splashing the young man. They didn't stay in the lake for long, soon running out to the searing heat of the fire. Juliana grabbed some blankets from the tent and the young man grabbed a flask filled with tea that they had made in preparation for their temporary icy existence. Juliana had been introduced to English tea in Brazil; the young man could drink it day and night. Juliana wasn't the biggest fan, but the young man absolutely loved it and she just liked drinking something warm. They were now huddled around the fire, under the sky which was an array of colours – oranges, blues, and purples – as the sun was setting.

Once they had warmed up, they lay in the opening of the tent, both lying in their sleeping bags, heads at the entrance. The fire still raged on, popping every so often with embers floating away into the night sky as they stared at the stars. They attempted to cook dinner from the comfort of their sleeping bags using long sticks that they could hold over the fire. Good idea in theory until the sticks started to break, so the young man and Juliana had to brave the cold. It was a little too cold for Juliana, so she brought over her sleeping bag and sat in that while she cooked. The young man just used the warmth of the fire to fight the cold, but when a nightly breeze came, his bones shivered.

When Juliana was asleep, the young man sat by the fire under the night sky and wrote in his diary.

"I have been thinking about my purpose lately and what I'm here on this planet to do, my reason for being. The essence of my existence and what I've come up with is pretty simple and god knows if it's any good, but I suppose I will find out. For me, my purpose in life right now is to explore and be free, to learn and grow. What my purpose will be in a year or ten years from now, I don't know, but I look forward to finding out. If it remains the same then so be it; I enjoy being in the moment and living in the now. If I don't, I might just miss this crazy thing called life. Our purpose in life isn't a fixed thing; it can be ever changing as we are ever-changing creatures in an ever-changing world. We must try our best to commit to the purpose we have today and what tomorrow will bring us, who knows. All I do know is, I can't say with certainty what my future will be, but I know what my present is and that is continuing this human experience of exploration, both physical and mental."

The young man closed his book and hunched over with his arms crossed he looking at the fire. His eyes began to close so he put a little more wood on the fire and crawled into the tent. Juliana was barley awake when she said, "You OK?"

He whispered, "Couldn't be better, my love."

"Good, I'm going back to bed, then."

Before he went off into a dream world, he took one more look at Juliana.

As the morning sun lit up the tent and slowly warmed the cool air inside, they woke up, the young man still half asleep. Juliana unzipped the opening of the tent – the fire was still smouldering with a tiny trail of smoke rising, now being all but a pile of ash.

She sat on top of the young man still wrapped up in his sleeping bag, and said, "My love, you need to wake up."

"Five minutes," he replied with sleepiness in his voice

"I'll tickle you," Juliana said

The young man was trapped inside the sleeping bag; this

made him perfect prey for tickling. He was crying with laughter.

"I'm up, I'm up," he cried with a big smile on his face. As he freed himself, Juliana ran out of the tent as she knew tickle revenge was coming. She took his boots to aid her escape and told him he could only have them back if he pinkie promised not to tickle her (between them, a pinkie promise was law and couldn't be broken). So, a truce was called, well, for now anyway, until he could get her at another time.

Later that day they trekked back to the tiny sea town where the boat was tied up at anchor and they bought supplies needed for their onward journey. As they began to sail the icy waters of the south Pacific Ocean again, heading for their next destination, they stood in wonderment just as they had the first time when sailing into the marina they saw the mountains which certainly were crafted by giants; they were masterpieces.

The young man and Juliana spent the next two weeks sailing up the Chilean coast and exploring this beautiful country. The rocky landscape of Chile's southern coast was spectacular and they even braved the icy water to go surfing a few times, but only a few as it was seriously cold.

Chapter 8

They were now on the open waters of the Pacific Ocean, Juliana steering the boat and the young man reading on the deck, sitting at the front with the wind blowing through his hair. Peru was the young couples' next destination, and they couldn't wait to get there as sailing had been rough the past couple of days. The young man and Juliana had had their first serious fight. The bad sea conditions hadn't helped and had made tensions high. They argued about a couple of things, one being the feeling of being on top of each other; they needed some alone time but neither wanted to hurt the other's feelings by saying so. Eventually things got under their skin and it came out in an argument. The second reason was that Juliana wanted to add her own style to the boat, make it feel like theirs, not just the young man's. But the young man didn't want anything to change; he had kept it the same way the old man had had it. It was the way the young man still connected with him; he could still envision the old man sitting on the deck drinking coffee in the morning sun. He hadn't told Juliana that, he'd just said 'no'.

Once the seas had calmed down, they still weren't talking to each other. The young man was looking out at the horizon and he remembered the lesson they had learned in Argentina. He

CHAPTER 8

realised they had broken one of the rules Santiago and Isabella had given them: never sleep on an argument. So, he went over to Juliana to settle it. It was hard for the young man as he was as stubborn as an old mule, but his love for Juliana was stronger. He told her he was sorry for being so dismissive about the idea of her adding her own style and he explained why. Then he said that this was their home and she should add her own style after all. He said living in the past wasn't good and the old man's interior design choices weren't the best – they both giggled at that, although Juliana tried not to as she was still upset. They agreed that having some time alone each day would be good; it was quite intense sharing a small space with someone. They made up quickly and it wasn't long before they were back to normal; Juliana couldn't stay upset with the young man for too long. They had argued before, but over silly things like what they were going to do, or what song to put on next. They had never argued like that before, but they dealt with it well; they talked about it, found solutions and said everything they were feeling. It can't get much better than that.

The young man and Juliana laid anchor off the southern coast of Peru. They went for a swim together, enjoying the sun as it set, and over dinner they talked about the world. The young man opened up to her about the inner workings of his mind, well, the best he could. Sometimes the hardest thing is to articulate the deepest thoughts that occupy your mind. She asked him to explain why he felt the way he did or why he felt lost.

The young man said, "I feel detached from this world; it doesn't make sense to me nor do I like it. I walk the streets and feel like I'm in a zoo, like I'm just watching people through glass windows and they are just surviving, content with existing, not living. I see things differently to them. I want to be free, free of this world, not trapped under this unexplainable thing I feel. The world before Delilah and the old man weighed me down. I was told not in these exact words but what they really meant was that in a simplified version, life went a little like this: education, job, marriage, family, retirement, death. I hated the idea of that. What kind of life is that? Mundane. I was told relentlessly by everyone that I needed to just get a career, buy a house, think of the future and none of that made sense to me. I don't want to work nine to five, five days a week until I retire. When I see this structure of life I see a waste of time. We don't have a lot of time to waste and if I'm to waste it, I want to waste it on sunsets and stars. I want to waste it on conversations with interesting people. I want to waste it on reading a good book. I want to waste it on making the world a better place and waste it on exploring a real human experience, my human experience. That's why I'm so happy with this life we're living together; we're free of these shackles I cannot bear to carry. I don't get people either. They truly confuse me. Why they enjoy the things they do, or why they are happy with their existence the way it is, why they don't ask deep questions, why they don't want to solve problems, why they don't see the world on its grand scale, why they do people things, why they participate in a system that has no real meaning. It's just a boring movie on repeat, that doesn't get better or worse the more you watch it. Or why they don't feel the same as I do – just confused about the structures we live within, the unwritten rules of our existence that we willingly abide by. I appreciate that these people also make the life we're living together great, but I still don't understand. I over analyse and think too much on a scale where my thoughts get lost. I may be a unique soul with unique feelings and unique thoughts. Maybe they're crazy, but they're mine."

After the young man had tried to explain his thoughts, Juliana smiled and said, "Thank you." They continued talking about it and realised that Juliana had quite a lot of the same feelings ; they were both just souls who hated conformity and normality. They were creatives and their minds needed space to be creative.

"I don't want you to think that I'm not happy," said the young man, "because I am. You make me happy, but I get pulled in two directions. There are my deep thoughts that are on a grand scale that make me sad and then my small thoughts that are comforting." With each conversation they had they grew closer. Juliana believed they were the same soul that was split in two and now they were together that soul was complete. She believed she had been destined to meet the young man.

The next day the winds had picked up and they flew along the coast. They arrived in the capital city of Peru, Lima. As they sailed in, they were struck by the sights of a city that sat on a natural god-like platform. On this platform sat a lighthouse which was a beacon for weary souls. The sun bounced off this magnificent rock formation that stretched for miles. The sun made it look bronze, as if they had just sailed into the kingdom of gods.

They walked the streets of Lima. The young man loved South American cities as they were explosions of colour. Each city seemed to have its own culture, customs, and traditions, but most importantly, food. All the buildings seemed to have their own personalities, dying to tell their secrets in the form of architectural riddles. Juliana loved eating and exploring local cuisine. She could spend hours searching for an ingredient or flavour which would spark an idea for her next food creation. She enjoyed cooking with the young man using local ingredients and flavours. So far, in all the places they had been, they had made sure to stock up on local produce and had experimented with cooking and making new dishes each night. The young man was still trying to work out Eithan's wife's secret recipe but he had still had no luck. However, with each attempt he felt like he was getting closer, and with each attempt he felt close to Eithan who he missed dearly. They regularly sent letters to each other, updating one another on the little things life provided them. The young man would read Eithan's letters on the deck of the boat, with his morning coffee while sitting on the old man's three-legged chair, Eithan read his letters whenever possible, mostly on the beach before he went surfing; he would contemplate the young man's words while he was on the waves.

The young man told Juliana he would take her to see Eithan one day. She was ecstatic as she had loved hearing the young man's stories about him. Also, she wanted to try Eithan's wife's secret recipe as she had eaten the young man's attempts way too many times now and needed the real thing!

While in Peru they had planned to go on a tour to see the Rainbow Mountains and Machu Picchu. So, while exploring the city, they went to the bus station to book the tour. They would leave Lima for Cusco tomorrow; from Cusco they would take a bus to the base of the Rainbow Mountains to begin the climb.

They wanted a change so they booked themselves into a hotel, a luxury country club in the centre of Lima. As they arrived to check in, they walked up the stone stairs which lead to the entrance. The stairs were beautifully shaped and got narrower towards the top. The balustrades were crafted into spirals that were supported by Roman-like pillars, the kind you imagine held up Olympus for the gods. The stone had an aged look to it; little specs of green moss were scattered all over. The stairs felt like a time capsule, and for a split second the young man and Juliana were transported to a sophisticated time of jazz and elaborate parties, with the illusion of walking up a staircase into a grand affair where they were to be welcomed by hosts and bands playing the most splendid music. The walk up the stairs made them feel the years gone by; made them feel the hundreds of people who had climbed the same steps. As they got to the top, the illusion ended but the grandness of the hotel remained. They weren't welcomed by hosts or a band playing the most splendid music, but they were welcomed by the most charming hotel manager.

Juliana wanted to stay in the hotel room for the rest of the day. She had been travelling with the young man for a while now, needed some time alone and wanted to pamper herself too. So the young man was kindly and lovingly banished from the room. He spent the day wandering and exploring the streets of Lima. On his walk he got talking to locals, as he usually did. They told him to check out Lima's street art; one of the locals he was talking to was the grandad of an artist who painted murals all over the city and he sung to the rooftops how great his grandson's art was. So, the young man took a walk, following the directions of the proud grandad, and as he turned a corner he was struck by an intriguing and alluring piece of art. It was a large portrait of a young man who was holding his face in his hand, and his head had a heart-shaped cut out where his face was. Inside that heart was a beautiful bird and behind that bird, in the background, was the dark of night. The heart-shaped face looked full of sadness and sorrow.

At first glance the young man saw it just as modern art, but with a closer, more intricate look, he saw the story the art was trying to tell him. For a second the young man thought about the beauty of art and literature, that it's beauty derives from the fact that each piece of art and text is completely unique for every reader or viewer. The same story will never be repeated; one piece of art becomes a thousand pieces of art. Each story becomes a thousand stories. The artist or author are merely architects of creativity. They provide the blueprints and narratives to spark a creative journey but the person absorbing the art and text has the power to define their own story; each little detail is a creation of their own imagination. Art and Literature allow everyone to become an artist and an author. For each person it means something different; it takes them on a different journey and leads them to a destination of their own choosing – that's the beauty of it.

The young man felt the art told him a story of hiding behind a mask. This particular person was in a dark sadness which the young man could relate to, or did he see himself in the artwork? But behind all that sadness was a beautiful bird that represented the real us, our truest self. If you peeled back all the layers of a person, the bird would be left, and it represented us at our purest level. The young man also saw how sometimes our beautiful bird could be trapped in a cage of our own doing; we allowed the ourselves to trap the bird and hide it from the world. We caged it up in the deepest darkest depths of our being; but how wrong we were to do so, as the bird was who we are, and the young man saw the man holding his saddened face as a symbol of freeing it. He saw it as a liberation, a rebellion against yourself, tearing away at the layers which had hidden the bird for too long. They were now gone and the bird could spread its wings and fly, to now be seen by the world.

After the young man had finished looking at the very emotional and thought-provoking art, he thought about whether he had a bird to set free. He paused for a few seconds in a state of deep thought and before he could answer his own question, a bird quickly fluttered out of a nearby tree. That immediately helped the young man answer his own question. Yes, he had a bird to set free. After answering his own question, he thought that everyone had their own bird to set free and an even deeper thought began to grow. He thought it would be amazing if everyone could open the cage and set their birds free. How amazing would it be if we didn't and others didn't put our birds in a cage?

He had been out for a while now and missed Juliana so he made his way back to the hotel. As he opened the door to their room, he could hear Juliana singing in the bathroom. This immediately brought a smile to the young man's face. The little things Juliana did always brought a smile to his face: her smile, her snoring, the way she danced while cooking and the way she cuddled him to near suffocation. They spent the evening together, curled up on the bed watching old movies and eating pizza. The young man loved old movies; he thought they were simply shot, yet captivating.

They were up before the sun rose to get an early morning bus. It was still dark outside and they quickly walked to the bus station as they were running a little late; they got to there with a minute to spare, Juliana saying, "Told you we would make it." En route for the rainbow mountains; they had been excited for this ever since they left Chile. They didn't plan much – only a couple of things they really wanted to do. They liked to use local knowledge and also wait to see how they felt once at the new location.

The bus journey there was bumpy, and the air conditioning

made you feel like you were in Antarctica. The young man and Juliana layered up with everything they had; so did all the other travellers. One person went to ask the driver if he could turn it off, if possible. The driver was either deaf or was very rude as he didn't respond. The lady walked back, shaking her head, to everyone's disappointment; the bus remained a freezer on wheels en route to Antarctica.

The journey was long – they were on the bus for hours but it felt like days, and the young man was getting a little grumpy towards the end of it. Juliana had the window seat; she had called shotgun as they walked up the steps of the bus. She liked to alternate between the young man's shoulder and the coldness of the window as a pillow. She teased him for being a little grumpy and started to pretended to tickle him. When that didn't work, she put the young man's Shackleton beanie on and started doing her English accent. The second she did this, the young man couldn't help but smile, although he tried not to.

Juliana, in an English accent, said, "I'm sorry to bother you, kind sir, but could this lady have a kiss, please?"

The young man, now laughing and beaming with joy, kissed her and took his beanie back. Now with the grumpiness gone, they looked out of the window and watched the world go by until they reached the next stop.

They had a small stopover in Cusco to get a quick bite to eat from a little food stall near the bus station that was selling guinea pig, a local delicacy in Peru. The young man and Juliana were hesitant to try it at first (a guinea pig seemed a little too innocent to eat) but soon hunger over took them and as they ate, they were surprised by how good it was. As they ate they got to know their fellow travellers a little.

CHAPTER 8

The young man, Juliana and all the other travellers stood at the base of the mountain stretching as they had been sitting down for hours, and waiting to start the hike up. They took a moment to compose themselves and bought ponchos from local venders.

The hike up was long but beautiful, in its own kind of way. The landscape was barren, a mountainous desert in the middle of Peru. On the last part of the hike, the mountains became striped in natural, yet strikingly bold colours. The colours seemed to go on for miles, stripe after stripe, colour after colour, they went down the side of the mountain, gradually fading away as they reached the bottom.

They reached the summit in good time. The tops of the mountains had a little snowfall on them and this only made the colours become bolder and more alive. Being at the summit truly took their breath away, both literally and figuratively: the altitude made the air thinner so everyone was breathing a little heavier, and the view figuratively took their breath away as it was simply stunning. They couldn't believe what was before them. One of the guides told them that a few years ago the snow melted due to climate change and when this happened it revealed the colours underneath. Since then, travellers and locals alike had come here in the thousands to see this natural wonder.

While at the summit, the young man and Juliana took in the view; the mountains were visual poetry. Once there, they had around ten minutes before they had to begin the climb back down. Some would say a seven hour round trip for ten minutes at the summit wouldn't be worth it, but the young man and Juliana would disagree. They had seen something unbelievable with their own eyes. They grew a deeper love for nature on top of that mountain. Soon they were climbing back down. Everyone fell asleep on the bus back to Cusco; the hike up and the fresh air had tired them out. Once they arrived back, having rested, one of the travellers suggested they all go out. Although sleep would have been nice, memories would be better. The tour guide showed them to the hotel. Everyone dumped their bags in their rooms and met downstairs ten minutes later. The night had just begun in Lima and the streets were crawling with people. They found a little bar where they talked, drank and laughed into the night until the bar closed, then made their way back to the hotel. It had a little garden where they continued their night, until one by one they went to bed ...

The next day quickly came around and they were to take another bus, this time heading into the Andes. They were going to follow the Inca trail to Machu Picchu; this part of the tour would be four days in the Andes. Once on the bus, nearly everyone fell asleep – the night out had left little time to be in the comfort of a hotel bed. The young man was awake for most the journey and he gazed out of the window, taking in Peru and her countryside.

The tour was going to take them four days as they needed to acclimatise to the altitude each day. On the third day they would make the big climb where the air would be getting a lot thinner and the mind would begin to feel strange. The young man and Juliana were worried about how they would deal with the altitude as they spent most their time at sea level, but the tour guide said they should be fine. The young man focused on him saying 'fine', but Juliana focused on the 'should' part.

On the first day they walked through the sacred valley, where locals still use Ancient Inca infrastructure. The young man and Juliana were blown away at the sight of the salt pools that went all the way down the mountain. The white pools took over the landscape and were hugged by the steep edges of the mountains on each side. Some of the pools were white, but quite a lot were creams, browns and greys. There were hundreds of these pools; they stood at the top looking down and couldn't see where they ended.

Before they got to the salt pools they had walked through villages and tiers of fertile farmland that went up the mountain side; these tiers looked like steps for giants. They stopped at one of these abandoned villages for a break and while they stopped, the young man and Juliana sat in the grassy hills overlooking the mountains and this ancient village.

Juliana said, "Maybe our giants from Patagonia helped the Incas build this!"

"I like the sound of that. I think you might be right," the young man replied with a giggling smile.

Juliana began brushing her boots through the long grass and then began to make her own music with them, tapping the toes together. The young man soon joined in and added a little humming of his own. Others from their tour group came over and joined in. The young man and Juliana smiled at them and they added some clapping and other sounds. Soon, half the tour group were overlooking the mountains making music, all adding random beats that echoed into the landscape. Then it ended, almost perfectly synchronised, and they all bowed and curtseyed to each other. Their break was over. The young man pulled Juliana up from the ground and they continued hiking through the ancient trail. Before they reached their campsite, they went through more abandoned Inca villages and hiked through more trails on the sides of mountains.

They stopped at the first campsite, where they had tents

waiting for them. They dumped their stuff in their tent, put fresh T-shirts on, and soon sat in a big mess tent in the centre of camp where dinner was being cooked for them. They all sat patiently around a huge communal table that nearly took over all the space in the tent. They discussed the day's events and mostly how sore their feet were. Dinner was served and the steaming bowls of goodness brough smiles to the faces and bellies of them all.

One of the people on their tour group was a Christian and began quietly saying grace before he ate. The young man wasn't a religious man but respected religion and what it meant to other people. He interrupted the group eating and said to the man saying grace, "Would you like to say grace for us all? That's if you all don't mind?" Nobody objected and they all put down their spoons. The man who was saying grace smiled at the young man and the young man gave him a little wink. Everybody took the hand of the person either side of them and then the man blessed the table. Although hardly any people at the table were religious, they all enjoyed it and it made the chill that came from a little gap in the tent go away. It brought the group closer and made the food taste that little bit better. After they had resumed eating, and said thank you again to the cooks and guides, Juliana took the young man's hand under the table and held it tight. She gave him a cute little smile that said, 'I love you'.

The man who had blessed the table said, "Being thankful and sharing that thankfulness with others is a simple tool that can help aid our happiness."

Nobody said anything, but all looked at the man and smiled; they all gave him a look of understanding. The rest of the evening was spent in the tent, talking and laughing at bad jokes.

CHAPTER 8

They had a meeting with the guides about timings for the next day and what to expect. To everyone's dismay, they were up well before the sun.

One of the guides got out a guitar and played a few songs. The young man, returning from a visit outside, was guided by the light escaping from the gaps in the tent and the sound of the guitar; the tent was a lighthouse guiding him to warmth and safety. Before going back in, he took a moment for himself. He closed his eyes while looking up, took a deep breath and smiled. The cold air tickled his nostrils as he breathed in. He took that moment to really take in where he was; he was in Peru trekking the Inca trail! But not just that, where he really was, was freedom. He kept reminding himself of this as sometimes it was easy to think he was in a dream and would wake up on that bridge again and would sink to the bottom from the weight of his burden. Then the young man opened his eyes and stared into the stars. Juliana came out to check on him. She stood in front of him and hugged him while also looking up at the stars.

A few moments later she said, "Hey... You coming in?"

"Yes... Just needed a moment to appreciate a few things."

They then went in to listen to the last few songs and sing along with everyone.

The night ended with the guides suggesting everyone get some sleep as they had a hard day ahead of them tomorrow. So, under their orders, they all walked out into the Peruvian night – these became speed walks the as the cold took them by surprise!

Everyone crawled into their tents. Before they went to bed, the young man and Juliana poked their heads out of their tent to gaze up at the Peruvian night sky but this time the young man didn't look up into the sky, he looked at Juliana. The young man thought the greatest adventure he could ever live would be in the eyes of Juliana. He thought for a moment as he looked at her that he could just look into her eyes forever and live the greatest life. Once she was asleep, the young man wrote, inspired by Juliana.

"If I could not see, but saw tonight, I would look at you for that good night."

He then closed his diary, closed his eyes, and drifted off into the Peruvian night.

On the second day the group continued their hike through the Inca trail. They hiked up the Dead Woman's Pass, which would be by far the hardest part of the journey, as it stood roughly half the height of Mount Everest, but would also be the most beautiful. They were in a valley where the altitude was gradually climbing. Either side of them, natural skyscrapers and the trail was lined with sun-dried shrubs. The tour guides walked around the group, checking on everyone and helping those struggling with the altitude. They walked through skinny trails that were only big enough for one; these trails had been flattered by the Incas who had originally laid them and by the courageous travellers who walked them today. Step by step the trail gets worn away and the crumbly path loosened with each passer-by. As they walked the trails, they looked down and saw the Amazon River from high above. They were told that it was the longest river in the world. The sounds of the river accompanied them as they followed the trail.

The group arrived at the next campsite after a hard day of hiking. They all craved some much-needed rest because tomorrow would be the climb up to Machu Picchu. The climb would get a little easier from here as the altitude drops.

The young man, Juliana and the group arrived at Machu

Picchu. The climb had been worth it as the view was beautiful; it was a city in the sky. To get to the now abandoned city, they climbed up some of the steepest and narrowest stone steps. On some of them, the young man and Juliana had to grapple up them. From the steps they could see the Amazon River flowing through the luscious forest below and the mountainous landscape the river carved its way through.

The young man and Juliana loved the idea that Machu Picchu was used by the Incas as an astrological observatory in the fifteenth century. They also loved the idea that before the telescope was invented, they went up into the mountains to better continue this human infatuation with the stars. But mostly, they loved that humans had most likely been looking up to the stars for eons and would continue to do so for eons to come.

Juliana said, "I can almost imagine them all sitting out here at night, watching and asking the question we all ask ... what's out there?"

The tour guides gave them plenty of time to explore Machu Picchu. They walked the ancient ruins and over looked them from a natural viewing platform above. The group spent hours exploring but soon came the time to head back down the mountain. However, not the way they had come up – they were going to take the train back down the mountain. The young man and Juliana boarded the train and found their seats, and the train started moving, gradually building speed. On the journey down, they weaved through the mountains, surrounded by green vegetation. It covered the ground and clung to the walls of the mountains and the hills. A river flowed next to the train; it could be heard when the windows were open. This was a very different experience to the one they had had climbing up.

The young man and Juliana took in the views from the train's many windows. They went for a walk through the carriages, all the way to the back of the train and they clung to the doors as they hung out of the carriage, wind in their faces, adrenaline pumping. While in the open, they felt a part of the mountains, as though they were a rare flower growing on its side. They leaned out of the rear windows and sipped on their drinks and not soon, a lady who worked on the train came to let them know dinner would be served soon. They made their way back to their seats, and over dinner the young man and Juliana, along with the group, toasted to what had been an amazing four days.

They arrived at Poroy station, then the last little bit of the journey was a coach ride back to Lima. Everyone, including the young man this time, fell asleep. Lack of sleep and a four-day trek through the Andes had caught up with them and their bodies just collapsed. They arrived back in Lima under the cover of night with the streetlamps warming the streets orange. Everyone had a few tears in their eyes as they said goodbye and walked back to their hotels. The young man carried Juliana the last hundred metres to the hotel entrance as she was so tired, and maybe a little lazy! But once she could sense her bed was close, she had a burst of energy and near enough ran up to the room, which made the young man smile. When he arrived at the room, he saw Juliana curled up on the bed, asleep, and he smiled. He closed the door, turned off the light, and crawled into bed next to Juliana.

The young man and Juliana had one more night in Peru. They were back in Lima and back at the country club, but not for long as they wanted to spend their last night there like locals, so they went to a little peña, which is a venue that plays traditional Peruvian music. The hotel manager had recommended it to them when they asked about what would be fun to do. The peña was small and packed. The stage was small; only half the band could fit on it. The guitars, flutes and bongos all played a beat that made the hips loosen and the soul unwind.

They went to the bar and had a drink. The young man raised his glass and said, "To us and this moment."

Juliana then clinked their glasses together and they drank. Standing at the bar, they took in the atmosphere and then walked onto the dance floor where the locals were wearing the tiles away. The young man and Juliana danced with the locals and followed their lead; the locals were proud to lead them. They danced with everyone, drifting from partner to partner; when the beat in the music changed, it was time to drift. The young man and Juliana picked up the style of dance pretty quickly and then let the music take control of them.

The man playing the flute on stage gave a wink to his band mates and that was the cue – he began freestyling and began a solo. He just played in the moment, seeing where he would be taken. Then the drums came back and got a little quicker and a little quicker, so the young man's hips did too. There was no structure to the dance; you just felt it and danced, no pressure to get the dance wrong as there was no structure. While dancing, the young man and Juliana couldn't help but think of Santiago and Isabella, and couldn't help revisit the memory in their minds of learning to dance in El Sonrisa on that empty dance floor. Everyone in the bar formed a circle, moving all the chairs out of the way. Pair by pair they would dance. The band moved to the edge of the circle. The young man was dragged in by a local lady and they danced, moving their hips and they worked their way round the dance floor. Then one of the band members clapped and that was the signal for the next pair to enter. The young man smiled at Juliana as she awaited her turn, then she was pulled into the circle and she too moved her hips to the sound of the drums which seemed to be going more quickly for her. She smiled and strutted around the dance floor; all the locals smiled and looked impressed as she was keeping up with the music. The lights from the ceiling shone down on everyone, heating the room; people stood by the open doors that led to the streets to cool down. A nice little breeze swept through the room.

After Juliana had danced, she stood next to the young man and watched as more and more people entered the circle to dance. Once everyone had entered the circle, the dance floor was free to be roamed again. The young man and Juliana danced with each other and just like in Argentina, the room seemed to empty for them, and all they could hear was the sounds of the band. When they danced, all they could see and feel was each other. After they danced, they had one more drink at the bar to hear the band play their last song of the evening and then they walked the streets of Lima back to the hotel. Once they got into the hotel they merrily danced and skipped through the hallways, trying to be as quiet as possible as they didn't want to wake anyone. When they got into their room, they sang songs in the shower together and ended the night on the balcony, watching the stars, talking about life, and cuddling.

Chapter 9

The young man and Juliana were sitting in the cabin going through some of the old man's stuff. He had an old battered box filled with photos, letters, and a couple of diaries. They were the last surviving relics of his adventurous life. The young man had heard many of the old man's stories but even a lifetime wouldn't be enough time to hear them all; these precious things were the last surviving accounts of the old man's adventures. One picture they found was labelled '1967 Morocco'. It was the old man, looking young in the picture, and a group of his friends posing in front of their van. The young man told Juliana about the stories the old man had told him before he sailed around the world. The old man had road tripped with some friends through Europe, heading south and into north Africa. He had been an adventurous soul with a hippie spirit. They looked at his pictures, passing them between each other; most of them were in black and white. They also read his letters and diary entries, trying to live his experiences through his words and pictures, which was quite easy as the old man was very detailed in his writing and took stunning photographs. The words and pictures transported them back to 1967. They took in turn to close their eyes so they could imagine what the old man had seen; one would read and, as the other listened, their mind painted pictures with the old man's words as the brush.

The old man had arrived in Marrakech, Morocco, after an eventful few weeks through Europe. On the last stretch of the road trip, the old man had fallen asleep in the back of the van, but he was woken by the sound of the exhaust blowing as the van came to a sounding halt. He sat up and looked through the window; they had arrived. The old man and his friends all jumped out of the van and ventured out into the dusty streets, all the buildings a peachy sand colour. They headed for the bustling market in old town for some food and exploration. The old man loved markets; he had grown up near Borough market in London and every place he went to he would also wander through the market. He felt you could really get to know a place quickly if you took a wander through the local market; you get a feel for local trade, traditions and food. Food is an important part of any culture and the old man was following the smell of food like a hound tracking a bird. He loved eating local and if possible, hearing about its history. The old man thought that food told a story, multiple stories with endless layers to unfold. He also thought that you could piece things together. If a society is made up of its culture and traditions, then food may just be the glue that holds it together. We share stories over food, we celebrate with food, we have dishes that sing to the essence of the land and what It provides us; food can provide a part of our identity.

The market was intense. The smell of spices filled the air. As the old man walked through, he saw vendors with baskets full of herbs that filled their stalls, bowls of spices that stood like spires. Colours were scattered around the market and beams of light shone through gaps in the sheets of cloth that were hung to block the sun. One of those beams of light shone on the entrance of a small shop. The old man was lured into the shop by the metallic mirrors, bowls and lamps that hung outside. As he took his first step in, he looked around and what had hung outside covered every wall in the shop. Light reflected and bounced. A man sat behind a tiny counter inside. The old man was very specific in his writing as he remembered the man on a stool, one leg crossed over the over. He was hard to see a first as the shop was filled to the last remaining space. One vendor had a wall of little glass bottles behind him. The old man asked what they were; he got no response from the vendor but he smiled. A local woman who spoke English told him they were traditional remedies that had remained unchanged for hundreds of years. The local woman also told the vendor what the old man had asked. Now the vendor understood, he got a few bottles down for the old man to look at. He hadn't intended to buy any of these bottles but thought it would be rude not to now, so with some help from the local women who translated for him, he bought one of the little bottles and then continued exploring the market.

The food stalls in the market brought life to the old man's taste buds; he bought a little from each vendor. The food all looked so good that the old man couldn't choose and his eyes began to get bigger than his stomach. So he and his friends all shared the food so they could all try a little of each. They moved from stall to stall, the smoke from each stall pulling them like they had an invisible rope around them. They all walked the market together a little while longer, until they could eat no more food. on his own. The old man drank tea in a little café he found on the corner of a small courtyard, in the maze-like streets of Marrakech. While drinking his tea, he soaked up the local vibe and wrote in his diary. The old man loved Moroccan tea, no milk just like he would have back at home. It came in a small glass and had a fresh mint leaf in it; it was comforting, like tea should be, but it was also refreshing.

The old man wrote:

"Marrakech is like a Russian doll – it seems to never end. More and more streets, more and more vendors, more and more moments that tingle the senses, more and more soul-warming people, more and more sunrises that I could watch for the rest of my life, and it will be a meaningful life. I have been to many places now and taken many photographs, and I fall in love with each place I go, but Marrakech, Marrakech has a unique charm unlike any place I've been before."

The old man was joined by another man who oozed imperialism. A man from a now ancient time, he wore a linen suit and had a little pocket square which he used to dab away the sweat from his forehead. The imperial man asked whether he would like some company. The old man loved meeting new people so happily welcomed him to his table.

As he sat down, he introduced himself. "The name's George," he said. Although he now knew his name, in his mind he had already named him the imperial man. They got talking and he found out that the imperial man had been living in Morocco during the summer for more than twelve years now. He quickly and openly shared his lavish lifestyle with the old man, telling him about his homes in Paris, Sicily, Budapest, London, and of course his house in Marrakech. But of all those, his sailing yacht was his most precious and beloved piece of property.

The old man said, "Well, all I own is what's in my backpack and one fifth of a van that, on most mornings, takes a lot of convincing to start."

CHAPTER 9

The imperial man asked, "Would you mind if I smoke my cigar?"

The old man was taken aback that he had even asked. A little under thirty minutes with the man and he knew he was as arrogant as they come, but shook his head, saying, "No, smoke away." He then picked up his glass and sipped at the tea.

The imperial man, before getting a match out to light his cigar, said, "Thanks a bunch".

The old man told the imperial man about how he and his friends had driven all the way to Marrakech. He was most engaged when the old man told him about his time in Paris, the imperial man having spent every Christmas in Paris with a few friends. He told the old man that he and his old war buddies' families would all spend it together, a tradition of many years now. After a long puff of his cigar and a thoughtful ponder looking up to the sky, exhaling he said, "I don't think I could do that, you know. When I come here I get the train; it is a much more pleasant experience." The imperial man had a pack of cards with him and asked whether the old man wanted to play. As they played, the imperial man analysed and watched the old man's every move, seeing if he was confident, good, strategic. The old man lost the friendly game of cards and afterwards, as he gathered his things and was about to leave, the imperial man asked whether he would like to come to a members' club later in the week – to play some cards and have a few drinks with him and some other gentlemen. The old man accepted his offer although he felt slightly uneasy as they had only known each other a few minutes over an hour. But the old man, being the free-loving hippie he was, chose to have faith and looked forward to their next meeting as he had never been to a members club before, so was excited for a new experience. The imperial man's last words were, "Make sure you wear a shirt." The old man left, disappearing into the streets of Marrakech which were like no other city streets he had walked before. As he walked away from the little café, the old man found himself down small side streets and while walking, for a second he thought, "Did I even bring a shirt?" He ran his hand along the crumbly peach walls, looked up and saw the blue skies. He then lowered his eyes, just a little and saw lots of windows with wooden frames that had small circle cut outs. These cut outs let the light fill the rooms when the shutters were opened. He wandered these side streets until he arrived back at the market. He had heard and smelled it well before he saw it. From there he walked back to his hotel, picking up a snack from a street vendor while doing so.

The old man and his friends were woken by the call to prayer each morning. The old man would get up to the call and sit on a straw-weaved chair on the rooftop. He had to climb up there, but once on top he would watch the sunrise. The Moroccan sunrise was the first the old man had truly watched; he had seen the sun rise before but had never taken the time to really watch the sun slowly rise, to slowly warm a city, to slowly bring life to the streets. The old man fell in love with the sun in Marrakech the very first time he sat on the rooftop; it was love at first sight and would be a love affair like no other.

The sun seemed bigger from that hotel rooftop; it encompassed the morning sky. Its warmth bounced off the landscape in the old man's view. The rising sun also made silhouettes of the buildings as it slowly rose in the sky. The old man would later bring coffee onto the rooftop. The smell and taste of fresh coffee with the sun slowly warming the chills from your skin was so simple but one of the old man's favourite things to do.

CHAPTER 9

This would come to be how he started every day – sunrise and coffee. If the sun was hiding, the old man would just close his eyes and envision it. But the old man told the young man that he and Ruby would always try and be somewhere in the sun. They would migrate to where the sun shone and the people were friendly.

The old man and his friends all shared a room; they were money-struck hippies looking for cheap adventure. They had shared the small van all the way there, doing hundreds of miles in it, so sharing a room was luxurious. The room wasn't special, two double beds and a bathroom, but it was cheap and clean, so they couldn't ask for much more; it was a royal place, in their minds.

They would all climb on the roof in the evening, the old man giving everyone a helping hand getting up there. They did this after the old man shared where he had vanished to for the last few mornings; they all said the call to prayer was too early, so they would all go up in the evenings instead. This worked for the old man as he enjoyed some time alone. They would all lay on each other's laps, forming a makeshift circle on the roof. They would watch the stars, sing songs, talk about how they were going to march to Parliament Square when they got home and protest the injustices in the world, but mostly they would just talk about love and freedom and how this trip was so far the greatest time of their lives. On one of the evenings up on the rooftop, they all fell asleep under the stars, still lying in the circle they had made. The call to prayer woke them all and, as the sun began to rise, the old man and his friends sat up and watched.

One of the friends said, "Now I wish you had told us it was this beautiful; it could never be too early in the morning for this!"

On the roof of that same night, before the sun had set and the evening came, they all sat up overlooking Marrakech, watching the market come alive in the evening dusk. The lights of the market stalls flickered on in sporadic bursts until they all lit up the soon-to-be night sky. The market's sandy coloured rooftops hid the jewels and the essence of Marrakech. Smoke from a food vendor effortlessly rose and blended into the night sky above. Dashes of colour were placed in view that showed a glimpse of what was hidden below but only a little as it seemed to be tempting you into its alluring wonderland that tickled the senses.

A couple of days had passed now and the old man and his friends were taking a quick road trip to the Atlas Mountains and would drive back tomorrow sometime. As they drove, one of the friends got out his guitar and began playing. He was taking requests but only the songs he liked, so in actual fact, he just played what he wanted which made everyone laugh. As they entered the mountainous range, they began driving through a luscious landscape with the backdrop of a mountain so high its summit was covered in snow. As they looked up and out of the windows, they saw the rugged and unforgiving landscape of the higher altitudes. They drove into the mountainous villages; being in the mountains was a welcome change from being in the city. They spent the day exploring: they hiked, drove in the mountains and were even invited for lunch by some locals who lived in the village. They fed the old man and his friends like kings. It seemed like every local who lived in the village had found out they were there and brought dishes to the old man and his friends. They all smiled at the locals and their hospitality and made sure to try a bit of everything so they didn't offend

CHAPTER 9

anyone. The old man and his friends were very trusting and never turned down random acts of hospitality; they loved locals and loved the time they spent with them. Luckily for them, they had always had an amazing and surprising time so far.

One evening later on in the week, the old man went to the club to meet the imperial man. He walked down a dusty side street and found the place. On the entrance door a brass sign read MGC in big, engraved letters and underneath, in smaller engraving, read it 'Marrakech Gentlemen's Club'. He entered the club and gave his name at reception. The receptionist checked the quest list then a host walked him to a table in the back of the club where the imperial man was waiting. A cloud of cigar smoke mysteriously hid him from the old man until it dispersed across the room.

The old man sat down. A waitress came over and placed down two glasses; the imperial man had pre-ordered drinks and had told them to promptly deliver them as the old man arrived. It created an environment of efficiency and control. The old man realised this but gave the imperial man the benefit of the doubt and to his surprise enjoyed the drink. They had a little small talk and once they settled into conversation, the imperial man wouldn't stop talking about his beloved boat. He kept going on about his love of it and how he would spend one month of the year sailing the Mediterranean. He also gloated about how he was one of very few socialites to have a boat like this or a boat at all.

They were joined by two gentlemen who sat down and called the waitress over to order some drinks. They introduced themselves – their names were Tobias and Alexander – then the waitress arrived and Tobias insisted on buying. He had had a very good night recently and wanted to return some of

Alexander's lost money in the form of drinks and a few laughs. Soon after the drinks arrived, they began playing cards. Luckily, it was the old man's game: blackjack.

As the night went on, the old man was down. They had been gambling on the games which the old man had been tricked into. The imperial man grinned at his cards, everything was going to plan; the imperial man hated free-spirited hippies – it went against his conservative upper classness.

The imperial man had made a few comments about the old man during the night but he laughed them off and tried to enjoy the evening. The other two gentlemen, Tobias and Alexander, were rather pleasant and enjoyed the old man's tales. They said to each other it was about time they went on a real trip.

In an act of arrogance, the imperial man, with superior confidence in the cards he had just been dealt, put his beloved boat up as a trophy prize to the winner of the last game of the evening. The winner would all come down to a shuffled deck of cards and a little bit of luck. The other two gentlemen were done – they didn't want any part of this last game. The old man, in their opinion, had been swindled out of nearly all his money and this last game was bound to take it all. They sat their drink in one hand, cigar in the other. A painstakingly slow ten minutes went by. The old man had a smile growing on his face as he looked at his cards. The imperial man saw the old man's smile and started rubbing his neck. He took a big swig of his drink and dabbed his forehead with his pocket square. For the imperial man, the room got a little darker, a little colder, the walls began to close in on him. He pulled on the collar of his shirt as he felt his arrogance begin to restrict his airways, the tie round his neck slowly began to feel like it was tightening. A thick trickle of sweat rolled down his neck. Could he have lost?

CHAPTER 9

The old man placed his cards down on the table. He picked up his drink, swirled it around a little and took a sip. One of the gentlemen watching took a puff of his cigar and blew out a cloud of smoke. For a few seconds the imperial man didn't know whether he had won or lost. As the cloud dispersed, the imperial man's heart sank. He placed his cards down and anger took over him. He began shouting, saying he had put the boat up as a joke. He laughed nervously and said that surely they knew it was a joke and that it was just a friendly game of cards. He also stated that it was preposterous and deemed it ridiculous that they were all taking the situation so seriously. He didn't think the old man would win as he had been losing all evening and now, because he had had one lucky draw of cards, he was going to win. He claimed how unfair this was.

The old man remained humble in his winning; he didn't gloat, nor did he even expose an emotion. This only added to the growing rage of the imperial man, whose anger was now growing by the second. The sweat that dripped from him seemed to be almost steaming. Deep down, the old man wanted to rub it in. He wanted to sing from the rooftops of the joy and pleasure it brought him to beat that wretched man. Luck had been on his side, he thought. The old man wasn't a religious man, but a believer in the universe. He believed if you put out good energy into the world, you would receive good energy, and in the old man's mind, this was him receiving good energy.

The imperial man began to refuse to give the boat away, saying how unfair it was and said, "What's that hippie going to do with a boat?"

One of the gentleman, Alexander, made a rather sarcastic remark. "Well, it is a boat so you never know, he may just sail her, George!"

The two gentlemen who were at the table told him he must uphold his debt; he couldn't break an arrangement. They said his behaviour was dishonourable and ungentlemanly. This really hit the imperial man's pride. One of the hosts came over when they heard the commotion. They tried settling the argument but couldn't get a word in. The club manger soon came over after the host had asked for his assistance in the matter. The manager wasn't happy as he didn't want anything to tarnish the club's reputation. Gossip would spread like a disease through the club; the club had founding principles which at this very moment the imperial man was breaking. The manager marched over and told the imperial man that he must honour his debts or his membership to the club would be stripped from him. He begrudgingly agreed to do this after his local prestige and socialite status was in jeopardy. One of the gentlemen that had been playing cards with them suggested the imperial man would show the old man the boat and provide all the documents he would need in a week's time. The gentlemen told the old man to meet him in Casablanca, specifically at the marina. The imperial man then stormed off, no handshake, no goodbye, just undying rage. The old man couldn't remember the gentleman's name so in his diary wrote about him as the 'gentleman'. After the dramatic events had concluded, the old man was given a complementary drink on the house and was also given an apology directly from the manager.

As the old man walked down the starlit streets of Marrakech on his way back to the hotel, he got thinking about what he was going to do with a boat. He couldn't even sail, but that was a problem for the future old man to worry about. Right now, he just enjoyed the feeling of winning the boat from that dreadful imperial man. The smells of cigar smoke and whiskey stained his shirt ...

Once he got back to the hotel, he told his friends all about the night's events and acted out how the imperial man had reacted and behaved which made his friends laugh. He told them how, for a few moments, the imperial man didn't know he had lost as his cards were hidden in a cloud of smoke. While telling his story, his friends were all squished together on the balcony, asking questions about what these people were like. They spoke of the rich upper class people like an alien race. The old man described them and the club. They all made fun of these posh people. The old man then found the last remaining space on the balcony to squish himself into and they all looked into the Marrakech night and spoke about their love of being a hippie and free. They also laughed at what the old man was going to do with a boat. All his friends said they would all drive down to Casablanca together in a week's time, but before that they were going to head into the desert for a festival.

The night before they were going to the desert, the old man wandered the market at night. The hanging lights from the stalls lit a path, the smoke from the food stalls carried the smells of meat and spices, people sat at little tables, mostly locals but a few travellers too. The travellers could easily be spotted because they all had one thing in common – they were all looking around with dazzled eyes and didn't know where to look, unlike the locals who sat and ate, for them this was home, and they had seen it a thousand times. The old man just wandered. He wanted to experience the market at night. He walked the path the lights lit up, taking in everything that was going on around him. He heard the sounds of food being grilled and the collected chatter of people. He saw people smiling and talking, he felt the wind brush against his skin and when he got close enough, he felt the fires from the food stalls warm him. And if he got really close, he felt that warm burning sensation grow until he had to take a step back to let the skin cool.

The day to leave for the desert had arrived. The old man and his friends got into the van which was sweltering. They quickly opened all the windows and they drove with the side door open, which wasn't a good idea as the wheels kicked up the sand and, in a matter of seconds, it engulfed the van. The van came to a screeching halt. The dust cloud inside was thick and you couldn't see the hands in front of your face. They all quickly exited, coughing. Once the old man he had coughed up a desert he began laughing. The laughter soon spread from person to person, with them each coughing up their own desert. They all sat on the side of the road in silence, waiting for the dust cloud inside to settle. No words, just shaking heads and smiles.

Once the dust cloud had settled they tried to brush as much of the sand out as possible. They drove into the desert and were met by some guides to take them further in for a few days before the festival started. They all wanted to experience the desert environment. They changed four wheels for four legs – they were to ride camels to where they would be spending a night under the stars in a traditional way.

The guides who led them came from a long line of people who lived in this harsh and unforgiving land; this was their home and their heritage. The three guides were all brothers who had started doing tours to bring more money in for the family and to share their culture with visitors. They rode camels into the desert, everyone wrapped up in scarfs protecting themselves from the midday sun. The old man enjoyed riding the camel. When they arrived at the campsite, the only respite from the heat was a big canvas propped up by stilts that had a vast array of small colourful flags hanging from it, which would have blown in the wind if here had been any that day. No wind, just a scorching heat. Once the midday sun had gone and it began to get a little cooler, the guides took them on a less traditional yet extraordinarily fun activity – they went sandboarding. The guides had made sleds and boards for them to all to use out of old wood. The old man, his friends and the three brothers all took it in turns to glide down the sea of sand, all laughing when someone fell off and rolled down. Their scarfs stopped the sand going in their mouths. At dinner, they all sat around the fire on the most beautiful handmade coloured rugs. While the fire raged and the food was going down with delight, the old man took a moment to look around at each of his friends and smiled as he thought to himself how happy and lucky he was to be travelling with them. The old man liked living in the moment; he found it brought him joy and allowed him to take in the finest of life's details.

The evening was a traditional Moroccan and hippie fusion: traditional food and customs with hippie vibes. The played guitar round the fire under the star-scattered sky. They softly sang their hearts out and when dinner had risen from the hot ashes it had been cooked in, they all sat round the fire in silence. The setting and the food deserved complete and utter attention. All that could be heard was the whistling of the wind and the crackling of the fire as embers flew into the night sky.

The old man slept under the stars. He used his bag as a pillow although it felt more like a soft brick that night, but it provided more comfort than the chilling sand would have. he thought about how he was surrounded by the vast expanse of the desert; the vastness gave room for the most audacious thoughts and dreams and the open space around him freed his mind to create and explore. The old man didn't sleep that night, who could with a view like that? He watched the stars moving slowly.

They arrived at the festival, and in the barren sand-swept landscape, a cluster of hippies had converged. The tents and flags had looked like an oasis from a distance. The heat waves that skimmed over the sand had blurred their vision but as they got closer, their vision gradually got clearer and they realised it was the festival. They didn't really know what to expect when they arrived, they had just been told about the festival from the young lady they'd picked up just outside Paris. She had told them they must go.

At this point, Juliana said, "Wait, do we have any letters or pictures from Paris? I would love to hear about this lady and Paris! I've seen pictures of Paris ... oh, I would love to go to Paris." They both rummaged through the box, papers and photos now scattered all over the table. Then the young man found more black and white photos and a couple of diary entries from Paris 1967. He began to read the old man's words; he could almost hear the old man's voice reading them to him. They were both transported and transfixed to Paris.

The old man and his friends had arrived in Paris in the early hours of the morning. A city of divine elegance, a city of beautiful architecture, beautiful people, beautiful food, and a city of enchanting streets that are best explored lost. These streets at night had lights that dazzled the eyes and awakened the soul. As they drove through these historical streets, the old man began daydreaming, having flashes of revolution, of resistance, of passion and hope. He vividly daydreamed of people gallantly marching on a fight to freedom, united as one for a better tomorrow. He envisioned people charging

CHAPTER 9

with the red, white, and blue striped flag against those who wished to hold them captive. Down the little side streets, he saw barricades of revolutionary resistance, muskets firing one by one holding off the blue jacketed soldiers of the French army. A few streets later they were on the road heading towards the Arc de Triomphe and the old man saw liberation; he saw the allied forces marching down the street after they had taken back Paris from forces of evil, hundreds of war-ridden men marching to freedom.

The old man and his friends sat in a little restaurant, only a matter of steps away from the Eiffel Tower. It stood tall and only came into view when crossing the road. The old man and his friends had walked through the park and found this restaurant. Little flower beds were outside each window and when a gentle gust of wind came, you were hit by a tidal wave of floral scents that tickle the senses. They ate, they talked, and they laughed. The owner of the restaurant came over to the hippie-filled table. He placed a tray on the table and handed out glasses and bottles. He put the tray under his arm and in his husky voice said, "I love laughter ... Music, laughter, and love is the antidote to pain and emptiness, my friends."

The old man said, "I like that – music, laughter and love." He looked at his friends and said, "We need to paint that on a flag for the festival."

The restaurant owner then said, "Those three things kept me going through the war. When all was lost, and emptiness ravaged my mind, those three things restored me."

From the window of the little restaurant the old man watched one of his friends run out. He ran over to a flower vendor, stopping cars in the street in the process. He brought some flowers then walked over to a lady. The old man and his friends couldn't make out what was being said but they were gripped, even the owner of the restaurant was gripped. He pulled up a chair to the group's table and sat to watch the events unfold. Everyone was entranced: people in the restaurant, people in the street even stopped to watch this passion-fuelled event unfold. For a few moments everything went quiet, everyone in their minds cheering on the moment, cheering on love. He gave the young lady the flowers and she smiled at the gesture. More words flew into the parisian air, then she kissed him on the cheek and the old man's friend began to walk back, beaming somehow with sadness and happiness. She had given a single flower back to him and on the way back to the restaurant he smelled it deeply and intently; he wanted to remember this moment in every way possible.

In the old man's eyes, watching this spontaneous act was like watching a black and white movie – no words, just movement ,and his mind ran wild with the possibilities of what was being said. The old man loved moments of spontaneity and in his mind, he would try and rewind it so he could watch it all over again. This black and white movie in the old man's mind was flickering like old movies used to.

As the friend walked back into the restaurant, he was greeted by clapping and cheers. People waved their hats in the air, the old man and his friends beamed. His friend stood in the doorway and bowed. He had just completed the most audacious task; he had followed the heart without the mind's consent.

A man who had watched from his car poked his head out of the window and passionately shouted, "L'amour est l'essence de la vie." He then turned to who they guessed was his wife and kissed her before a car behind them tooted and he drove off, waving his hat out of the window.

CHAPTER 9

The old man's friend sat back down and drank his coffee. He looked at the flower, he looked at each petal, each fibre in each petal – this flower was a symbol of his heart's wishes. The old man asked what the man had shouted through his window; the owner of the restaurant told them it translated into English as "Love is the essence of life." Soon the old man's vision went back to colour and everybody who had stood still to watch continued about their day.

That night the old man got lost in the Parisian streets. He went for a quick walk but found himself walking for hours. He followed the riverbank, he sat in the park and looked at the Eiffel Tower under moonlight, while it glimmered and shone with its lights. He then thought how beautiful Paris must be from up there, so he got the elevator up to the top and what he saw was so stunning that words couldn't do it justice. There was only the old man and an attendant on the viewing platform. He must have been there a while as he was told he would have to go down soon. On the way down, he looked through the window, looking up and down, trying to take it all in. Paris at night had a charm, like most cities do, but with Paris the old man found it different. The nights were special and grew new life. As he walked, the streets poetic montages flew through the old man's mind.

On the way out of Paris a young lady was on the side of the street holding a cardboard sign asking for a free ride to Nice; was a hitchhiking hippie. The old man and his friends stopped for her. Although they had little to no room, they welcomed her aboard, the old man tied her bag to the roof with all the others off they went. She introduced herself to everyone; her name was Amelie. They told her about their end destination of Morocco and she lit up with excitement. She told them they must go to the festival in the desert, and that they would be there at the right time! She had gone herself two years ago. Amelie described it as being like riding a wave of transcended freedom, while having ...

Everyone took turns driving the van and while the old man took his turn, he stuck his hand out of the window, gliding it through the air, feeling the wind being sliced by his fingertips. Sadly, their time with Amelie was over. It had been short but sweet, and they dropped her off in Nice where her boyfriend was waiting for her. They did stop for a quick chat with her boyfriend and said that maybe they would see them on their way back.

The young man was handing more photos to Juliana from the box. "I can't believe we're only just going through these now!" she said.

"I know," replied the young man. "The box was hidden under the bed and the old man never told me about them, but I think it's more exciting this way. There's a sense of the unknown and you never know, we could uncover something."

Juliana smiled at the young man's words and then a thought popped into her head. "What if the old man was a spy or was in the mafia? Actually, no, from the pictures I've seen of him he looks more like a pirate." The young man was now crying with laugher at the thought of the old man sailing the open seas as a pirate.

At the festival people were playing music, talking, they were dancing to freedom and just shared vibes with a community of like-minded souls. Some of the music was rehearsed and some was in the moment experimentation; individuals would get on stage with or sometimes without an instrument and see where the moment would take them. People expressed their

CHAPTER 9

freedom in any way they wanted. Banners and flags of this hippie wonderland glowed in the sun.

A man on stage performed an acoustic cover of a classic which sparked a conversation between the old man and some others that would take them surprisingly around the world as, two of the guys had just come off the hippie trail. They had driven from Amsterdam to Bangkok and were now in Marrakech. One lady was telling the group about her travels through the Mediterranean; the old man's eyes dilated, ears heightened at her words. He fell in love with her words and her beauty, drifting between them, unable to focus on both or one for too long. She told stories of an Italian road trip and island hopping in Greece.

Sitting in a circle, under one of the many canvases, sand in everyone's hair, the old man and the lady had locked eyes. She began to slowly play with her hair; she had two flowers placed over each ear and a leather weaved headband. He had never seen anyone so beautiful; his heart trembled at the sight of her chocolate brown hair, red cheeks that had been kissed by the sun, her eyes greener and more enchanting than a rare emerald that had been dug up from the red earth of Africa.

The old man smiled at the lady as she got up and began to walk away. He didn't want her to leave and was trying to build the courage to get up and talk to her. Just as he was about to get up, he realised she wasn't leaving; this beautiful flower-powered hippie skipped and twirled round the circle to the old man. Everything blurred except for her. She stood over him like the goddess of freedom and love and the sun glowed around her. The old man was speechless. She smiled in an adoring way, then sat down and leaned into him lips nearly touching, noses gently brushing together. She slowly took a flower from behind one of her ears and placed it behind one of the old man's. No words had been exchanged yet, only eye contact. The lady then whisked the old man away; the day was taken by love and the spirit of the desert.

The old man sat with the lady. The heat of the Sahara put them in a trance, the heat waves danced for them, moving over the sand like belly dancers, the sand tickled their feet, the desert whispered words to them. They danced, they meditated, they sat in silence in each other's company, they philosophised, they became one with the earth. The lady and the old man had been granted access to nirvana; they had no worries of past or future, no desire or pain. The desert had granted them a rare freedom. They spent all day in this rare freedom and at the end of the day, they lay in a sandy hill next to the festival and watched the sun set together

When the desert night came, the old man and the lady walked back to the tents. The night air had cooled the sand from its scorching past; fires around the festival warmed the night. All the hippies gathered round the multitude of fires to share an evening meal together. The old man met up round one of these fires with his friends who all had stories to tell, stories of new friends, new perspectives on life, new experiences and mostly of love. Everyone had fallen in love at the festival; it must have been something in the food or the atmosphere. They all spent the rest of the evening dancing round the fires and making new friends.

Juliana looked at the young man, excited and curious "Wait, is the lady in the letters Ruby?" she asked.

"No," said the young man. "The old man told me he met Ruby in Istanbul a few years later. He never told me about this lady he met."

CHAPTER 9

Juliana said, "The old man had enough stories to write a thousand novels. This one must have slipped through."

The next day was another day in the desert spent in lucid freedom. The heat of the day had dried the small amount of moisture in the air from the night before. The lady the old man had was infatuated with and had hastily fallen in love with had vanished; she was now but a memory. The old man walked round the festival asking anyone he saw if they had seen this lady; no one had. He was heartbroken but his friends were there to lift his spirits.

When the old man realised he wasn't going to find the lady he had spent lucid freedom with, he distracted himself with his camera, taking pictures of people and moments. He was unaware how the pictures would turn out, as they had to be developed. The old man thought half the fun came from not knowing what you had captured and it kept him in the moment, focusing on the moments.

The young man stopped reading for a second and said, "The old man was an artist with a camera. He never edited any of his pictures. They were left the way they were captured ... Did I ever tell you that the old man and Ruby had an apartment in western Berlin during the Cold War? It was an old warehouse that had been converted to a living space. The old man had a darkroom where he would develop his pictures!"

"That's so cool," said Juliana. "I bet they had big windows that let lots of light in, perfect for painting. Did you ever get to go to the apartment?"

"No, I didn't. The old man sold it when Ruby died and moved back onto the boat."

"That's a shame," said Juliana. "Was photography a hobby of his or did he do it for a living?"

"It was a passion that was also a living," the young man replied. "He did all sorts of work. He did a little photojournalism and would write articles for newspapers, but he didn't really talk about it that much. I'm guessing he took pictures that needed to be taken but were also hard to take. But he did talk about the apartment in Berlin a lot though."

"I would love an apartment like that!" said Juliana.

After the festival had finished, they all drove down to Casablanca to meet the imperial man and see the old man's new boat. The drive down was exhausting; the old man and his friends hadn't had much sleep the past few days and the heat sapped any remaining energy out of them. When they weren't driving, they were drifting in and out of . They had driven through the city to get to Marrakech but didn't stay – just a short stop for petrol and food– so they were excited to explore their new surroundings for the time they had in the city.

A long drive later they got to the marina and met the imperial man. He was accompanied by one of the gentlemen the old man had played cards with that night; he thought the gentleman had come to make sure the debt was honoured and to make sure the imperial man acted in a polite and gentlemanly manner. But even so, the imperial man still tried to persuade and argue his point that it was unfair he had to hand over the boat because he lost a game of cards; he played the victim as if he had been hustled. As he pleaded his case, the old man and his friends couldn't help but admire his tenacity; he fought for the boat until the last second. Eventually the accompanying gentleman stepped in and assertively reminded him he that must uphold the debt and the imperial man reluctantly handed over the papers. The imperial man walked off in a childlike strop, while the gentleman shook the old man's hand and wished him a good day.

The old man and his friends stayed on the boat and looked around it. They sat on the deck and came up with ideas of what their friend could do with the boat; most of them suggested selling it. He, too, had thought selling the boat was the best option, but that was before he saw it; after that there was no thought of selling any more – but what do? he thought.

The old man sat at the helm of the boat, wondering what to do. He gripped the wheel began to think about the places they could see together. The old man wasn't ready to stop travelling, he wasn't ready at all. He had had a taste of lucid freedom and had been to nirvana. In that very moment he had a realisation of an urge to explore and be truly free. But his thoughts were interrupted by a local man asking if he were the new owner of this beauty.

The old man replied, "Yes, I am."

The local man introduced himself. "My name is Abbas."

The old man welcomed him aboard and they began talking. Abbas asked the old man how such a young man could afford a boat like this; he assumed the old man came from money. But he was surprised and delighted to hear the old man's story of winning the boat from the imperial man in a game of cards. Abbas had never liked him although he had always been nice to him and loved the beauty of the boat. He told the old man that the imperial man had always looked down on him for being a fisherman and a working man. They knew he had come from money; he had never worked a day in his life and that was probably the reason why he looked down on people. The old man told Abbas that the imperial man had called the boat 'property' in a previous conversation. The look on Abbas' face was a look of disgust.

"She is not property," he said. "She is art. She is so much more than wood and sails; she is a feeling of exploration and freedom."

The old man smiled. "Beautifully said."

They continued talking and Abbas told him that his name meant 'lion' in Arabic. His father told him, "A lion is courageous and to make it in this world, we must be courageous like the lion."

The old man then jokingly said, "My name's Richard and it means Richard in English."

Abbas smiled and laughed at the old man's sarcastic remark. He then offered to teach the old man to sail. The old man liked the idea – the way he spoke about the boat and it encapsulating the feeling of freedom and exploration resonated with his desire for nirvana. He had only just met Abbas, but he seemed like a good honest man. He offered to pay him for his time but Abbas refused; he said the pleasure of getting to sail this beautiful lady would be enough and he invited the old man to his house for dinner that night. They spent a little longer on the boat, admiring its craftsmanship. Abbas slowly ran his hand along the edges of the cabin, walked slowly round the boat and made his way back to the old man.

"May I?" he asked.

"Of course," the old man said.

Abbas gripped the wheel at the handles, he rubbed his thumbs over the top and then gripped it a little tighter. He smiled and said, "She truly is a beauty." He knelt down, looking out to sea, with his hand on the deck of the boat, before walking back to the old man again. Before Abbas went home, the old man told him about his friends and that he thought he would like them.

CHAPTER 9

Before the old man could say any more, Abbas invited them to dinner as well.

"I want to hear all about you and your friends' adventures over dinner. Now, my friend, I will see you later. My wife will be wondering where I am and I need to tell her we're having guests."

The old man sat at the front of the boat, rocking gently with the waves. His friends soon arrived back and on time. Once they all clambered aboard, he told them about Abbas and that he had invited them all to dinner tonight. They were all excited as they loved meeting new people and eating food.

When the evening came, the old man and his friends walked to a rocky formation that made its way out to sea. The rocks were large and they hopped between them, the waves spraying a mist over them from time to time. The old man and his friends got to the end of the rocky formation and they all stood arm in arm with the sounds of the waves smashing into the rocks and the spray settling on their skin. No one said a thing, but the silence was like one big hug. They hopped back over the rocks and arrived at a little beach house. Two knocks on the door and Abbas' smiling face greeted them into his home. They were all introduced by the old man to Abbas, whose wife soon came out the kitchen and introduced herself.

"Hi, I'm Delilah," she said.

They sat in a small dining room; around the table they were all nearly touching shoulders. Delilah came in and out of the room, putting dishes on the table. The room became more and more alive with each dish; she had served a feast. Everyone was hoping they could eat soon as they stared at the food already on the table, but Delilah kept bringing more dishes. Over dinner, Abbas and his wife told them the story of how they met, and they all got lost in the story.

Delilah was an English teacher who came over after the war to teach and met Abbas at the market a few weeks after she had arrived. She went there every morning to get fresh produce, and Abbas was there every morning delivering some of the fish he had caught to local vendors and restaurants. For a week, Abbas only smiled at Delilah. One day he plucked up the courage to go up to her, but all he could say was, "Fish?" Delilah had seen Abbas' smiles and had smiled back; she found him cute and infuriating that he wouldn't come and talk to her. She accepted the fish he offered her, and walked away with a smile on her face. The next day Abbas finally had the courage for a real conversation. They talked over some tea on little stools (or wooden crates!). Delilah laughed at all his jokes and Abbas listened intently to all her stories, each word she said, he fell deeper and deeper into her eyes. After tea, Delilah had to go to the school, so Abbas walked her there and asked whether he could meet her once she had finished for the day. She smiled and said she would like that. Abbas met Delilah after school every day and what had been intended to be a couple of months in Morocco for her ended up being forever. They had fallen in love under the African sun. Although they were from different worlds, it didn't matter; when two souls collide, there is no stopping it.

The rest of the evening was spent eating more food and drinking more wine. The old man and his friends offered to wash and dry the dishes, and while doing so, they watched Delilah and Abbas. They were just sitting at the table, sipping wine and talking but they were so in love.

The evening ended and the old man and his friends were walking along the beach when one of his friends said, "I really want to jump in the sea." They all looked at each other giving a look of 'oh we're doing this!' Devilish smiles grew on their faces and they started running across the sand, tearing off their clothes, throwing them in the air. Once they reached the water they dived in and swam in the moonlight. The walk back was wet and salty. They all dried off outside the van and slept in the old man's new boat, which now had wet sandy foot marks on the deck.

Eventually the old man's friends had to go. They had spent the past couple of months together travelling and had stayed for as long as possible, but they had things planned back home. The old man had things planned too but he had a change of heart and wasn't ready to return home yet. He told them he was going to stay a little while longer and then, with a little luck, travel the world. He had a boat and some money kindly provided by the imperial man's arrogance. Life had provided him with an opportunity he couldn't refuse.

They drove off, heads out of the window waving farewell. One of the girls was wearing a flower crown which began to leave a trail of petals floating in the air as they were snatched by the wind. The old man caught one of them and rubbed it between his thumb and finger. He wondered when he would see his friends again or see the grassy rolling hills of the English countryside. Abbas put his hand on the old man's shoulder; the heavy grip grounded the old man's thoughts, it settled a racing heart, it settled an anxious mind. The old man had spent the last four months with his friends, so it was a sad moment saying goodbye.

The old man spent another couple of months in Casablanca learning to sail. He and Abbas would sail every day of those two months under the Moroccan sun. But before the fun could start, work had to be done. The old man helped Abbas on his fishing boat. In the evenings they would lay out the nets in the pitch black, the only light coming from the boat's floodlights which lit the water around them; the light would move as the boat rocked. The old man loved Abbas's boat and there was one spot that would squeak if you put your foot in the right place. With a smile, Abbas would say, "No squeaking, more fishing." In the mornings the old man and Abbas would be back out to sea to pull in the nets and collect the fish they had hopefully caught. Abbas only took what he could sell or eat himself, everything else was thrown back in the sea. Abbas was naturally and morally inclined to be an environmentally friendly fisherman and would teach his practices to anyone who wanted to know. He always told the old man, "Look after the ocean and all those that live in her and she will look after you." He also said, "Don't think of the ocean as just water. She is so much more than that; she is a living breathing organism that needs to be taken care of." Abbas let that sink in for a moment and then added, "I don't know whether I'm just a lucky man or the ocean knows I care for her, but I have never come back ashore without fish."

The old man didn't really know what to say but replied, "Well, I will make sure to take care of her on my travels, the best I can." Abbas smiled and patted the old man on the back in a fatherly manner.

While fishing, the old man also took pictures. If he had a moment, he would capture it. He was building a collection of photos from his time with Abbas and Delilah. He thought about calling the collection 'spirit of the lion'. When he wasn't fishing, learning to sail or taking photos, the old man wandered and explored and on the odd occasion, daydream. He would dream of the desert where he had experienced nirvana with the lady who vanished.

Little did the old man know at the time, but Morocco would be the birthplace of many of the habits that he would take into old age; his morning coffee with a sunrise happened every morning in Casablanca on the deck of the boat or the doorstep of Abbas' and Delilah's house. At the end of the day, when they had sailed and fished, Delilah would serve the most delicious food under the Moroccan sky. On most days, they ended it in the garden with a drink and would go over the day's sailing lesson. They told stories; Abbas liked the old man's stories of growing up in London and the old man liked any and all of Abbas' stories. But Delilah always had the best stories, and after a glass of wine, also had the best jokes. The old man and Abbas fished every day apart from Saturdays; Saturdays were reserved for Delilah. Abbas and Delilah spent the day together walking the markets. They had lunch together in their favourite restaurant, walked along the beach and danced around the house. The old man and Abbas still had their lesson on Saturdays but it was a shorter lesson. Delilah came along and helped sail too. Abbas and Delilah had grown fond of the old man. They had two children but they were grown up and living their own lives now, so they found themselves mothering and fathering all those they could help.

The old man's two months soon came to an end and it was time for another farewell. He soon came to find that goodbyes got a little easier –but this one was going to be hard. On the day before the old man was leaving, he blindfolded Abbas and Delilah and guided them down the jetty to the boat, telling them he had a surprise for them. He pulled off their blindfolds and revealed the new name of the boat: the back of the boat read,

Delilah. The old man then presented Casablanca's finest in budget champagne to christen the boat with. Abbas wasn't an emotional man but had one tear fall from his eye. Abbas smashed the bottle over the bow of the boat – it was now ready for a voyage around the world. Abbas patted the old man on the back. He loved this tribute to their friendship. With Abbas and Delilah on the boat, they all toasted to the new name and to the old man's safe travels. They had one more evening together before the old man left and they spent it doing nothing special, just some good wine between friends sitting in the same spot in the garden, watching the sunset together.

Before the old man left, Abbas gave him a gift – a three legged chair which had been his for years. The old man had told him that he loved the chair weeks ago. It was unique in that it originally had four legs but Abbas fixed it. The old man loved the quirkiness of the chair and it turned out Abbas wasn't just a good fisherman, he was also a good carpenter. He wasn't a rich man nor a poor man, he got by OK. He told the old man that he needed a chair to sit in on his deck while he had his morning coffee and he needed something to remember him by. The old man said he would come back and visit as much as he could. Abbas and Delilah waved the old man off on his adventure. The old man kept his promise to Abbas and retuned to Morocco dozens of times over the years and when he returned, he would help out on the fishing boat.

The young man placed the old man's diary on the table and looked at a black and white picture of the old man, Abbas and Delilah, on the boat. He and Juliana sat back and smiled, going over the old man's African adventure. The old man had had the coolest stories, the coolest vinyl and the young man reassured Juliana he had had the coolest beard.

Chapter 10

The young man and Juliana had now left Peru and South America and were heading for the tropical central American nation of Costa Rica. They were going to sail along the coastline for as long as possible, before heading out across open water. On the first night of sailing they laid anchor off the coast off Ecuador. Just as the sun was setting, Juliana went for a swim. She liked putting her eyes in line with the water. The sea turned golden with the glowing of the sun. The young man sat on the deck of the boat in his hammock reading a letter from Eithan. Eithan told the young man about his surfing, and a big wave he had caught a few days ago. He'd wished he were there to witness it and surf it with him, or he jokingly added, 'you could just fall in while I surfed'. He told him how the kids and his wife missed him and how they couldn't wait to meet Juliana one day.

The young man, still in his hammock, began writing in his diary. Juliana sat next to him on the deck drawing in her sketch book. He wrote:

"I have been travelling now for what feels like a lifetime; my travels have changed me. I can't really explain it, each person I meet, each place I go adds new perspectives and I feel a new appreciation for life. But I don't know how to really explain it, all I know is I feel different and I like it. I've come to realise that I love the little things like a beautiful view, a sunset, a conversation, and good company. For me, it's the small things that make a place or a moment special and memorable. As I write this, I'm looking at my love, my best friend, my partner in crime and can't help but smile. My life is much better shared with her. And Juliana, if you're reading this, which I'm sure you are, I love you. I think about the old man regularly but today I was really thinking of him, and if I were to have one more moment with him, I don't think I could find the words to say how grateful I am for his friendship, his words, his warmth and mostly for saving my life. I've been thinking how crazy is it that one little thing or moment can change the course of your life, like me jumping off the bridge on that particular night, at that particular time made me and the old man meet. And without jumping, I never would have met Juliana! I never would be writing this sitting on my very own boat in the Pacific Ocean. I do try and remind myself to remember how lucky I am to be travelling and how lucky I am to have been given a second chance by the old man."

They were a couple of days away from Costa Rica. When they arrived, they intended to surf and explore the country's luscious national parks.

While the young man was sailing, Juliana sat at the side of the boat, feet dangling over the side, getting splashed by the waves that tickled her feet when they met. They were only a few miles from the coast of Costa Rica now. She was looking through a pair of binoculars and every once in a while, she would glance over her shoulder to get a look at the young man. He was carried away sailing ...

They arrived at a small marina that had a medieval feel to it, as it was built up with stone walls to protect the boats from the chaos of the ocean.

The young couple spent the day surfing on a beach not too far away. The young man carried the surfboards; Juliana carried the bags. On the beach they set up; a worn red blanket was a shield from the scorching sand, a small speaker quietly playing music and a little cooler box was filled with lunch. When they weren't sailing, they were telling tales of days gone by and dreams of days to come.

The young man remembered all the old man had told him. Towards the end of their time together, the old man, over a morning coffee, started the day with a lesson. He told the young man to always have a childlike spirit. He said that this spirit is often lost as we get older and become more serious and wound up under the pressures of life. The old man believed that it kept the soul alive to explore with a childlike sense of curiosity, to try new things, to laugh, and laugh at yourself, play games and be yourself. All of this will add to a happier life. The young man could remember all the old man's words of wisdom. He could close his eyes and be back on the boat on with him, sitting with him listening to a life well lived and he could even sometimes close his eyes and picture the old man in his three legged chair giving him some fatherly advice on life and everything in between.

Later that night, back at the boat, they were reading, Juliana in the hammock, the young man lying on the deck with some cushions. They caught eyes with the owner of a massive yacht, and he raised his drink to them almost as a toast for one, being sailors, and two, sharing this magnificent marina with each other. A little later the man walked over with a lady and, standing on the jetty, introduced themselves.

"I'm William and this is my wife, Arabella." The young man welcomed them aboard. He stood up and Juliana gracefully spun out the hammock and offered them both a drink. They all sat on the deck. Juliana got a blanket out as the wooden deck was chilling from being slowly cooled in the night air. They began talking about life and the shared stories of their battles with the ocean. William and Arabella loved hearing about the humpback whales everything about the young man's and Juliana's story. Arabella's heart throbbed; she loved the feeling of love and youthful adventure. William loved the visuals of the young couple sailing around the world, chasing freedom and life. William told the young man how much he loved the boat.

The young man jokingly said, "Well, we can swap boats, if you like?" They all laughed.

"Don't tempt me," William said.

"This boat is over fifty years old," said the young man. "The old man I told you about, who left the boat to me after he passed, had won the boat in a game of cards in Marrakech in 1967. After winning it, he sailed her around the world. She's sailed in every ocean, been to every continent and still looks good as new ... Oh, I love this boat."

"Now that's a story," William said. "So you wouldn't be here with us right now if the old man hadn't won a game of cards In Marrakech in 1967?"

William turned to Arabella with pleading eyes. She knew what he was going to ask; he wanted to ask if they could get a boat like the young man's.

"We can talk about it later," she said.

He smiled – half the battle was won. A little later into the evening, they left. The young man and Juliana went into the cabin to play some cards before bed. He kneeled at the end of

CHAPTER 10

the bed and Juliana lay snuggled up under the duvet facing him, both falling asleep not too much later. The young man had to slowly get into bed so as not to wake the sleeping beauty.

The next day the young man and Juliana went cave diving. They were excited as, although they had been diving few times, they had never cave dived. As they were on the small boat going to the dive location, they were a little anxious as they knew they would be in some pretty tight spaces. Juliana and the young man were side by side on this boat and she was gripping his hand tight, but also secretly in between their legs as she didn't want the other divers to know she was nervous. They fell backwards off the boat when instructed to and they followed the dive leaders into the opening of the underwater maze.

A few minutes into the dive, they swam into an enormous chamber. The chamber had the same feel to it as the opera house in Argentina had., It evoked feelings of grandness, although this chamber gave a sense of a forgotten world that had been swallowed by the ocean too. Beams of light struck through little cracks in the rock above, like the spotlights of the opera house displaying the beauty on show. When they entered the chamber, they encountered tropical sea life. Beautiful electric lemon coloured fish with green racing stripes lined the walls of this underwater world. There were hundreds of them swimming in unison, skating against the walls of the cave. The young man and Juliana had never seen wildlife so colourful ...

The dive leaders let all the divers spend a few minutes in the chamber taking it all in, they all looked to be in confused astonishment. How could something so beautiful be in an underwater cave? The dive leaders used these few minutes to check all the divers' equipment, as the next bit they were going to swim into would be a bit smaller, enough room for about two divers at once. When the young man and Juliana saw the gap they would be swimming into, their hearts began pounding; they would be sweating if they weren't under water. For an unexperienced cave diver, it felt like being buried alive, their chests felt a little heavier. But once they were in the gap and their anxiety had calmed down, it opened the door to take in the beauty; the ceiling had rock formations that looked like melted chocolate dripping down. One chamber they entered had a natural Greek palace-style column. This chamber was also close to the surface so when the divers looked up, they could see ripples on the water's surface when water droplets fell from the vegetation above. The young man and Juliana continued following the guide rope they were instructed to hold while in the tighter spaces, and while swimming they took in the unusual surroundings. There was less wildlife in the tighter spaces. The sights they were seeing were alien-like; the rocks had calcified and a large pillar in the middle of this small chamber seemed to hold up a bed of needles that looked like they were slowly dripping down. The young man and Juliana turned the head torches on their helmets on. They lit up the chamber, adding new colours and perspectives.

They made their way back through the underwater labyrinth and began to rise back up to the surface, where they peeled off their masks and rubbed their eyes, beaming with joy. The instructor, who was on land, looked at all the heads bobbing in the water. He smiled at them and shook his hand with the rock star gesture; this was an acknowledgement of how cool the experience was and how cool they were for doing it. Once they were out the water and the gear was put away, they all drove back to the drop-off point, shaking the water out their ears.

Later the same day the young man and Juliana were met at the marina entrance by a man in a polo shirt and white shorts, who told them they were invited to dinner aboard The Charlotte, that was William and Arabella's boat. The young man and Juliana knew they couldn't turn up to dinner in sea-worn clothes, so they quickly went into town. Juliana picked them both something out to wear while the young man went to buy a bottle of wine as a dinner gift. They quickly rushed back to the boat to get ready then walked over for dinner, only a little late.

William and Arabella welcomed them aboard and gave them a quick tour around their palace of a boat. They guided them to the upper deck where they had a table ready overlooking the small marina. Dinner, of course, was as luxurious and perfect as expected, a surprising five courses. The young man and Juliana felt like royalty for the night as they had never had more than three courses. Over dinner, Arabella asked the young couple if they would like some advice that she wished everyone could follow. The young man said, "Please do." They both sat up a little straighter in preparation for Arabella's words. Her eyes lit up like fireworks and as she looked into their eyes.

She passionately said, "Be a rebel ... Life is short so take chances. You don't want to live a life of what ifs and regret. Say yes more and roll the dice of life; you will win some and lose some but at least you're playing!"

William interrupted and said, "Being a rebel also means not following the crowd. It means making your own path, choosing the path least followed. You need to live a life of your choosing; don't allow someone else or a society tell you how to live your life. You only have one so make it yours, be a rebel."

"I love that," said Juliana. "I've always had a feeling like this but didn't feel like it would be accepted, and that I would become outcasted."

William said, "You may be outcasted, as people find it hard to rationalise something that they could never conceive themselves. You will be a rogue among conformists, but there are so many potential rebels out there. It's just people are scared – they allow fear to take over. Being a rebel isn't easy, but nothing easy is worthwhile."

Later in the evening, William and Arabella asked the young couple if they had any plans for the next day, and if they didn't, would they like to go on a day trip with them? They said they would keep the day a surprise but told them that they would be getting in a helicopter. After dinner, the young man and Juliana walked back to the boat, excited about the following day. They had never been on a helicopter before. William and Arabella said it would be better if they didn't know what they were going to do; the eyes and the imagination needed to see it together.

As the young man and Juliana settled down for the evening they turned on the boat's fairy lights which hugged the beams and wooden frames. Then moved onto the wooden deck and danced under the stars. Nothing spectacular, just a little two step. Juliana had her head resting on the young man's chest, their hands interlocked, holding each other tight and every now and again they gripped each other a little tighter.

"I love you," said Juliana. "I'm so happy … I can't believe how lucky I am to be dancing under the stars with you. I can't believe I'm travelling the world with my best friend and love. This very moment will be written in the stars forever, just like all our time together. We will be written in the stars."

The young man held her tighter, lifted her chin, brushed her hair behind her ear, brushing her cheek while doing so, then kissed her.

"No, I'm the lucky one," he said.

She smiled and they continued their dance. The night ended lying beneath a moonlit sky under a blanket with them sharing a not so cold beer.

The next day came swiftly around. The young man and Juliana were up early, anxiously awaiting the day ahead. Their minds were racing thinking about what William and Arabella could have planned for them. Over their morning coffee they bounced around ideas of what they might be going to do, each one seemingly getting more ridiculous. They had been instructed last night at dinner to be at the marina entrance for seven a.m. sharp.

They got there for six fifty-five a.m. and five minutes later a black 4x4 pulled up to take them to William and Arabella. The journey wasn't long, only a quick drive to an opening in the forest. Waiting for them was a helicopter with William and Arabella outside. As they got in, William handed them some headphones to wear. They felt the weight of the helicopter slowly lift off the ground – it wasn't a natural feeling, both their stomachs felt a little funny. This time the young man was gripping Juliana's hand tight. Just as Juliana had done he held her hand in between their legs as he didn't want William and Arabella thinking he was scared.

Chuff, Chuff, chuff, chuff.

As they flew over the Costa Rican jungle they were awestruck by its beauty and couldn't help but think what it must be like to be bird seeing this every day. What must it be like to be a bird? When they thought of a bird, they thought of freedom. It all seemed so small and peaceful from the sky. A twenty minute flight later they began their decent to the jungle floor. They landed in what seemed like the Garden of Eden, complete and utter paradise. Once the helicopter went silent, all that was left was the crashing sound of a waterfall that was not yet visible and the brushing sounds of the trees moving in the wind. The young man and Juliana swam under the waterfall and in the pool of water below. The young man, feeling adventurous, climbed along a rocky path up to a naturally made platform that had a tree growing through it. The roots had cracked the rock and they also provided good grip as the rock was wet and rather slippy. Without hesitation, he looked down then jumped, floating through the air for a few long seconds to then plunge into the pool of icy jungle water, the little pockets of air beating him to the surface.

Arabella had planned a jungle lunch for them all, a banquet of fresh fruits and local cuisine. The young man and Juliana had never seen so many different types of fruits; they could peel them apart with their bare hands and the juices dripped off their fingers.

They had got to know each other quite well now. The couples sat opposite each other at lunch. William and Arabella wanted to give the young couple some more advice.

William said, "Staying humble and being grateful are important skills to have. Being humble will keep your ego in check and staying humble will make you realise that no matter how much money, how much power or how high you are on a social hierarchy, you are merely human and when you put yourself in the grand scheme of things you are irrelevant. I don't mean this to sound pessimistic or be a negative outlook on life. It should be a relief to know that staying humble will set you free. Being humble will release you from the burden of ego. We're on this spinning rock for a very little but precious amount of time. Our state of temporary existence is what makes life so great and our irrelevance sets us free to follow our dreams. Being humble is a modern superpower and our ego is what deprives us of this power."

After one last swim they dried themselves off and once again got on the helicopter to go to the next location on William and Arabella's itinerary. Again, feeling as free as a bird, soon a large mountain appeared but as they got closer, William told them, "That's no mountain, it's a volcano." The young man and Juliana had never seen a volcano, not much different from a mountain apart from mountains don't have the potential to erupt with lava. William asked the pilot to fly as close to the volcano as possible.

Juliana said, "You've got to be joking."

William said, "Trust me."

As they got closer to the volcano's summit they began to peer inside and what they saw was surprising and left them both with questions. They expected to see searing red lava but what they saw was what looked like a pool of steamy milk. William was surprised, too, as he had never flown over the volcano before. It left them all perplexed.

They descended once again and this time the helicopter landed in an opening in the jungle, where another 4x4 was waiting for them with a uniformed man. William and Arabella let the young man and Juliana know that they were heading to the Cloud Forest Biological Reserve. Arabella let it slip she, too, was excited. William just smiled and shook his head – he was wondering how long she was going to last before she told them. To his surprise, Arabella had done quite well; he thought she would have told them the whole thing a lot sooner.

William looked at the young man and Juliana and said, "You're going to love this."

They had to drive into the jungle to get to the start of the tree top walkway. As they became tall as trees and walked like giants through this dense forest, they couldn't help but think of what William had told them earlier about being humble.

The young man looked at Juliana and said, "Doesn't the forest make you feel small?"

"Yes," she replied. "I feel like a grain of sand on the beach."

The young man then said, "I think I understand what William meant earlier. We are so small. All of this was here before us and will continue to be here after us. Staying humble helps us live a more meaningful life."

Juliana smiled, took hold of the young man's hand, and said, "I'm really glad we met William and Arabella."

They continued walking as giants and they got to a viewing platform which rested high above the forest. From here they saw little pockets of clouds which were sporadically dotted all over the forest, all looking like balls of cotton wool. The jungle went on for what seemed like forever and the viewing platform had given them all a welcomed relief from the humidity of the jungle. Only the four of them stood high above the trees, and from up here you could hear the jungle singing you songs.

As they made their way back through the jungle, they saw some of the wildlife that had been doing the singing. They enjoyed seeing the birds and monkeys, but neither the young man or Juliana were keen on the idea of seeing any insects or bugs.

As they drove back to the opening where the helicopter was waiting for them, the sun was beginning to set. The blades began turning and they were off. The young man and

CHAPTER 10

Juliana had never seen a sunset like this before, not from the perspective of the gods. Juliana told William and Arabella about how the young man, every night without question, watched the sunset and looked at the stars. William then told the pilot to fly a little higher, so he did, then higher again. William smiled looking out the window and whispered to himself, "Now we're flying."

As they began to rise, the young man could see the sun kissing the horizon; they all watched the sunset.

William said, "The flight back to the marina is going to take a while."

"No worries," said the young man. "Got any stories?"

"Yes," said William. "I'll give you my story, if you want."

"I'd like to hear it," said the young man.

William then went on to say, "My story starts off as I became an orphan at the age of 14. Getting thrown around foster parents, I caused a lot of trouble and I eventually ran away and needed to provide for myself. So I set up businesses and the more money I made, I used to set up new businesses. They continued to grow and I didn't stop. I had the mentality of needing more – because I didn't have my parents anymore I used material items to give me happiness. But that lead me down a rabbit hole as I then always needed and wanted new things. I never had enough. I was always chasing something out of reach. I became obsessed with having more, material things became more important than relationships as I was so scarred from my parents' death. Years went on by and I became a cog in a machine of my own making. Then I went on a business trip to India. At first it was only meant to be a week, but it ended up being a two month trip. On the third day of my trip I met Arabella. She was a free spirited traveller on a yoga retreat. We bumped into each other by pure chance, a few seconds sooner or later and we may have never met. We spoke for what felt like hours but in actuality was only a few minutes, but she had to go as the bus was waiting for her and that was it, she was gone. On my last day in India I had an urge I had never felt before; I wanted to break away from my routine and travel. I think it was meeting Arabella; those words we exchanged unlocked a door in my mind I didn't know I had. So I decided to take a chance and I went on a trip across India. Over the next two months I travelled India, from the desert of Rajasthan to the blue city of Jodhpur to the Taj Mahal to the tropics of Goa. For the first time in my life I wasn't thinking about work, or money. But I eventually had to come back to reality, and I had to get on my flight. Once I was home and back at work, I felt empty. It didn't feel the same anymore. India had left me a changed man. So, I decided to stop running my businesses full time. I hired new CEOs for the businesses and took more of a backseat role so that I could have a more balanced life. A few months passed, and I decided to go back to India and guess who I saw at the airport? Arabella! She was heading home. I couldn't let her get away a second time so I asked her if she would want to travel with me, and to my surprise she said yes. So, we bought a van and went on a monumental drive across India and all the way across south east Asia. We spent months travelling and at the end of the trip, I asked Arabella to marry me. Now, to really cut a long story short, we now travel the world and are working on our foundation. It's crazy how one little thing can change your life; me simply meeting Arabella changed everything. When I get down and sad, like we all do, I try, no I make myself remember how lucky I am to have met Arabella. Life has unexpected moments that surprise us and can change our destiny. We all have them, it's just taking them."

The young man said, "That's an amazing story, William." Arabella put her head on William's shoulder, embracing him for his tender retelling of their days gone by. The setting sun made the helicopter's cabin glow and as the sun began to set, the air began to get cooler and crisper. The sun was a few moments away from hiding for the night

Once they landed, the same 4x4 which dropped them off was awaiting their arrival to take them back to the marina. On the drive back, Juliana fell asleep on the young man's lap, using his hoodie as a pillow, snoring away. Arabella and the young man looked at each other and smiled – it was a silent conversation acknowledging her cuteness.

By the time they got back to the marina, the sun was hiding and the darkness came out to play. The young man and Juliana said goodnight to William and Arabella and thanked them for what had been an amazing day. They said they didn't know how they could repay them.

William then said, "Stay in touch. Keep us updated on your travels and we can meet you guys someday off the coast of somewhere."

Juliana quickly responded, "We're not leaving just yet so we can meet up again, if you would like?"

"We would like that very much," said Arabella.

The went back to their boat and the second their heads hit the pillow they were asleep. The swaying of the boat and the clinking of the metal on the sails moving in the wind was a lullaby of some sorts.

The young man and Juliana spent the next two days exploring the local areas, and in the evenings met up with William and Arabella to watch the sunsets and star gaze. Once the sun had set and they were alone, they danced with the moon as their witness. The young man and Juliana liked spending time with William and Arabella as they could see themselves in both of them. It gave them hope that this fairy tale love would never die. Something Arabella had told Juliana while William and the young man were walking ahead stuck in her mind. She had told her, "If you feel like you're ever drifting apart or all seems lost, you just need to fan the embers so the fire can burn once again. But I have a feeling you two won't ever need to do this."

Juliana just smiled and said, "You think so?"

"Couldn't be more sure if I wanted to," replied Arabella.

The young man also saw hope on a more personal note. William was a living, breathing example, a symbol of hope that you can go from emptiness and darkness to fulfilment and light. The young man had a fear that he was living in a temporary bubble, and that eventually that bubble would pop. William gave him hope that he wasn't in a bubble and that he too could continue this life-changing trajectory he'd been on since the old man pulled him out of the river. His biggest fear was that someday he would end up on another bridge with the rain pouring down and this time there would be no old man to save him. William made the young man realise that life is merely the choices we make, and those choices can be good or bad but no matter what they are, they are ours and ours alone. If the young man wanted to continue living this life, he had the power to do so. The bubble would only pop if the young man himself held the needle; the needle is a choice and to pop the bubble is a choice.

William said, "There are some things in life that are out of our control and for these situations the only choice we have is how we react and adapt to these situations. We are never completely powerless."

The young man smiled and told William that the old man had said the same thing to him in the letter he left. William paused for a few seconds, looking at the young man with sympathetic eyes, and said, "Well, he was a wise man." Williams words comforted the young man's anxious mind about what the future held for him.

On one of the evenings they spent with William and Arabella the young couple taught them to dance. They had started a bonfire on the beach that lit up the sand and warmed the night air.

The young man just told them to, 'head to the fire'.

William laughed and said, "What if there's more than one fire?"

"Well, you might meet some interesting people, but we'll look out for you and wave."

They sat on the beach waiting for William and Arabella to arrive. Juliana was dancing around the fire when she saw them in the distance and waved them over. As the figures got closer, they began to wave back; it was them. After a little catch up from the day's events, the young man took Arabella's hand and Juliana took Williams, both leading them in the dance of the tango. William was a little hesitant at first and said many times he wasn't much of a dancer and that he would happily watch, but he got a look from Arabella with her soft gentle eyes and William couldn't resist those eyes, so he began to dance with Juliana.

They danced with their bare feet in the ground, trousers rolled up, with nothing but the sound of the waves and the crackling of the fire to accompany them. No music, on this occasion the silence added an intimacy to the dance. After Arabella and

William had learned enough, they swapped partners. The young man smirking at Juliana in a charming way curled his finger at her, enticing her into his arms. She ran into them. He lifted her into the air and held her there for a moment, then slowly put her back down and elegantly flowed into dance.

The night ended with them lying in the sand, sharing a bottle of Arabella's favourite wine. With that bottle of wine gone a little later, they played a rather amusing game of charades until the night took them in its arms and they slept like babies under the star skattered sky. The fire gradually burned out in the hours that followed. They were woken by the rising of the sun, all except the young man. He was already up and had made his way to Delilah. They were wondering where he could be, when he appeared in the distance walking down the beach, flask and cups in hand. The young man had the sun behind him and it made him glow. He looked like a saviour, on a mission to save their sore heads; the cure, coffee. William was too hungover to enjoy the sun and laid back down in the sand. The young man placed his coffee next to him. The rest of them, all sleepy eyed, drank their coffee in silence with the waves crashing in front of them. The young man had also brought his surfboard with him, and after he drank his coffee he stripped off down to his trunks and paddled out, the morning sun warming his skin. He closed his eyes and embraced it all. The young man ran his hands in the water and over his board, then cupping his hands he filled them with water and splashed his face. This was a ritual Eithan had done for many years; he felt it connected him to the ocean and would make him surf better. So, the young man did it; it connected him to the ocean and Eithan. After the ritual, he turned the board facing the beach and the forest and then he paddled until he caught a wave. He rode that wave like he was the wave. He felt everything slow down until he was back sitting on the board.

It was that time again; the young man and Juliana were off. They left the comfort of the marina for the open seas once again. They continued sailing up the central American coast exploring what all these culturally unique and stunning countries had to offer, falling in love which each as much or if not more than the last. They spent the next few weeks doing so ...

Chapter 11

They had spent weeks sailing up the central American coast and were heading for Mexico City, Mexico. They were in a marina in Guatemala. William and Arabella were near the area and said they would be happy to look after the boat for the young man and Juliana, on one condition – that William could sail Delilah. The young man was more than happy to let William do so, as long as Delilah was returned in one piece. The young man and Juliana were going to catch a flight to Mexico City for a few days to experience the Mexican festival, the Day of the Dead. Before they went, they spent the evening with William and Arabella, and over dinner told them their new stories and showed them pictures of places they had visited since sailing up from Costa Rica.

After they returned from dinner with William and Arabella, the young man sat at the back of the boat, trousers rolled up a little with his feet dipped in the water writing in his diary. He wrote:

"I'm sitting here, the sea air giving me goosebumps. The pages are flapping in the wind. While sailing today I had an idea for a poem in my mind, I was writing it in my head as we sailed along the coast.

'Don't be beaten into submission, the light in life is the light you shine. March, march, march to the beat of the drum of your heart. Your life is yours; your life is yours. Beware of those who have accepted submission, for they have accepted the average, the mundane. They have given up on the beauty of isolation, the isolation of being able to live fully, to love fully. When we aren't beaten into submission, our isolation sets us free and our boldness and willingness to shine our light in the shadows'.

The more I travel and the more people I see, the further into the realm of the unknown I go."

The young man and Juliana rose the next morning, not knowing what to expect from Mexico City. They had read a lot about the place, but there was a big difference between reading and experiencing, so they were itching to go. It was also a nice treat to be going on a plane; the young man had never been on a plane. He was extremely nervous before take-off and also a little excited. He tried putting on a brave face, but Juliana knew he was nervous so held his hand. But once they were in the air, he was fine. They both ordered a drink and settled in for the flight, which to their delight was smooth all the way, no trouble, no turbulence, no crying baby to get passively aggressive at.

As the plane began to make it's decent, the young man began to get nervous again. He buckled his seat belt tight and gripped the armchair with force, all while feeling tense. Juliana gave a caring smile and placed her hand over his. But with the screeching sound of the types on the tarmac, the young man became more relaxed and once they had stopped he just smiled at Juliana and her small gestures of compassion.

They were now in Mexico City and took a taxi from the airport; they made sure to agree a price with the driver beforehand, so they didn't get scammed. The drive into the city was hot and sticky. The windows were cranked open but were broken so only went down by a couple of inches. It seemed as though the air conditioning was broken too. The driver was instructed to drive them into the town centre as the young man and Juliana needed to find a hotel to spend the next couple of days; the driver had recommended a hotel where his brother worked. Once the driver had got their luggage out and he was paid, they wandered the streets with their backpacks on. They hadn't packed much as they hated lugging lots of luggage around. They arrived at a few hotels but they were all fully booked; they should have known as it was a big festival. They spent a few hours walking the streets of the city, going from hotel to hotel. Eventually they arrived at a boutique hotel which luckily had one more room available and with even more luck, happened to overlook the street where the parade would be going down. So, they paid in full and went up to the room. A young worker carried their bags and showed them their room which was like a sauna. The young man and Juliana were both pouring with sweat from walking the Mexican streets for what felt like days. They opened the door leading to the balcony and a cool breeze slowly gushed in, bringing a refreshing chill over their skin.

The hotel room made them feel like they were in Mexico. Some hotels have a mundane feeling, but not this one. The room sang from a hymn sheet of Mexican essence: the walls were peach coloured, the curtains were hot-rod red, the floors were polished concrete, the ceiling had its wooden beams exposed and the bed was a deep mahogany with intricate carpentry in the headboard. Both of them ran their fingers over the carving and into the grooves. Flowers had been carved with life-like accuracy, which they would later find out was done by a local carpenter who had been working from the same workshop for all of forty years. The young man and Juliana could feel the love he felt for his work – the bed told a short story of the carpenter's soul. A grand staircase led up from the front deck to the first floor where the young man and Juliana's room was. All the rooms in the hotel had different coloured doors and theirs was baby blue. Every detail had been carefully thought out and had been creativity fused with the building; the young man and Juliana had never been in a hotel with so much character.

Juliana had gone down to reception to ask a couple of questions. She said she would only be a minute but the young man knew she would be gone for longer than said that; Juliana loved talking and especially to new faces. She got talking to the lady at the front desk who was telling her about the festival. She told them they should get costumes and dress up. The lady at the front desk was also a make-up artist and offered to do their make-up for the festival. Without a second thought, Juliana said yes. The receptionist's name was Maria. Maria was off on the day of the festival and asked Juliana if later on in the evening, they would like to come to a party. It was a large party held every year in an old factory, now turned club. Juliana thanked her for the offer and said she would talk to the young man and let her know a little later.

Later in the morning the young man and Juliana went out to buy some costumes for the festival. The young man wanted an all-black skeleton tuxedo and Julian wanted an old emerald green lace corset dress. After a morning of scavenging for their costumes and an afternoon of exploring the city, they were exhausted and had dinner in the hotel's restaurant. All the dinner tables had candles and the shiniest cutlery they had ever seen; it was the finest and simplest details that made this hotel simply wonderful. After dinner, the remainder of the evening was spent in the lounge, with the staff listening to one of the waiters play the piano. All the tables and chairs were up and they all sat around listening intently. They talked, they laughed, they drank; it was a perfect ending to a long day.

The day of the festival arrived. Maria knocked on the young couple's hotel room door. She was already dressed up in something similar to Juliana – a sleeveless deep blue corset dress. She started doing their make-up and they spent the early morning listening to music and watching the people swarm to the streets in preparation for this beautiful celebration. Maria told the young man and Juliana that the festival was about remembering loved ones who were no longer here and celebrating life.

She said, "In Mexican culture, we believe death is just a part of life. It is to be celebrated as the dead are awakened and we celebrate with them. The Day of the Dead festival is celebration."

As they left the hotel and started walking, they were struck by flowers and memorials that lined the streets. As they walked a little further up, a small green came into view. It glowed Biblically, with people gathered round, lighting candles for loved ones who had passed, connecting to them through their love. The smell of perfectly curated flowers danced in the air. A young girl came up to the young man and tapped him on his shoulder. She gave him a candle to place down with all the others. He stared into the flame for a few moments, captivated by its simple yet powerful potency; the young man could look into a flame or fire forever. He began to think of the old man. Juliana gripped his hand with both of hers; she knew he was thinking of the old man. He was happy at first thinking of the time they had shared and the memories they had made but then a sadness came over him when he thought about the old man never meeting Juliana or not being able to share their tales of travels over a cold beer on the deck of Delilah. But then he took a deep breath and felt Juliana's soft hands holding him tight and remembered what Maria had told them, that this was a celebration. So, he placed the candle down among all the others and smiled at the memory of the old man, almost hearing his voice telling him he was proud of the man he'd become and the man he was yet to become.

Before the parade started, the young man, Juliana and Maria went to find a good spot to watch the parade from. After a short wait, they heard the unified beating of the drums. The energy grew rapidly, people were excited for the parade to begin. Children ran over to their parents, climbing onto the shoulder of whichever parent or grandparent they found first. A boy on the shoulders of his father looked so happy, he had his face painted and had a cheesy grin. He kept hitting his father on the head, making sure he was seeing what he was seeing. He looked down to his father, seeing him upside down giggling and laughing. He kept pointing at all he was seeing and his father stood with a smile on his face from the joy of his son.

All the performers were dressed up in colourful skeleton costumes, and all their faces had been painted like skulls with sharp black and white features, but the parade had more colour than the young man and Juliana expected. All the women had beautiful floral headpieces that were set in different arrangements and were unique to each lady, giving them a beautiful sense of individuality. The smell of gunpowder from the fireworks lingered in the air, and combined with the flowers that lined the streets, made an aroma that was surprisingly pleasant. The smoke from the burned-out fireworks dispersed across the dusty streets and from that smoke, skeletal characters emerged, putting on a display that was enchantingly and mysterious. The music from the parade made the characters come alive in a display of deathly theatrics.

Some of the skull masks the performers were wearing were huge. They were like large puppets as they controlled their movements with wooden handles. One of the skeleton characters had an old English top hat on, another was made to look like old Indian chief with a colourful feather crown , while others just had skeletons that expressed colour. As the performers walked the streets they waved at the crowds and while dancing they threw flowers into the crowds. The streets were full of life and colour. Flowers, candles, and confetti lined the streets, which were dusty and dry and somehow when the dust was kicked up it smelled like chillies. It was confusing, but the young man liked it. It clung to your clothes and just when you thought the smell had gone, a gentle gust of wind would awaken them and remind you they were still there.

The young man and Juliana took a break from the festival up in the hotel room, As they walked into the hotel the sounds of the parade followed them, now a little quieter but still ever so present. They opened the doors and stood on the balcony and watched. From up here it was electric. The parade was still moving and from the balcony you could still smell the chillies. Leaning on the balcony, the young man and Juliana saw a lady took centre stage in the parade. In her presence, the candles seemed to dim down for her. There seemed to be no noise; all went quiet as she gracefully and eerily drifted down the street. This lady was dancing in the presence of death with love in her heart and with each wave of her arm, with each step she took, each movement she made, it all came together to create a performance that would be carved into the living for the dead.

CHAPTER 11

She wore a black dress and had the most fluorescent hat; a varying array of flowers and feathers covered the hat that burst with colour. The inside glittered and shone, bouncing off the light from the candles that lined the street. Flowers were also placed on the lady's shoulders. All of this emphasized the lady's face which the young man and Juliana thought was strangely beautiful, considering her face was painted like a skull. Her eyes were a piercing blue. The young man and Juliana watched this lady studiously. She danced with a flow that was soothing and elegant. From the moment their eyes locked onto her it felt like time had frozen. Everything around her was motionless as she elegantly moved down the street. Her dance was mesmerising and put everyone who watched her in a temporary trance-like state. A violinist accompanied the lady, walking behind her playing a melody of equal class and beauty.

The Day of the Dead festival was more than the young man and Juliana had expected; they expected it to be more morbid and darker with slow music and more emphasis on the sadness of death and mourning. But what the Day of the Dead turned out to be was a vibrant celebration of life! Maria had told them a little of what to expect but sometimes the eyes need to see before they can believe.

Once they had cooled off in the hotel room, the young man and Juliana walked back out into the street. As they stepped out of the hotel door, they saw a young boy and girl dancing next to them, inspired by the performers, and they brought smiles to everyone around. The next group of dancers they saw danced with extreme authority. They didn't ask for your attention – they took it. The flames that dimmed down and bowed for the lady burned brighter and stood to attention for this group. They all moved as one and their feet marched to the beat of the drums as they moved down the street. All the men wore pinstriped trousers, white shirts and multi-coloured sombreros; they all dressed the same to add an essence of unity. The women were all in vibrant dresses and wore flower headdress. They moved their dresses how a bullfighter would wave his cape in an arena enticing a bull. Each flick and wave of their dresses drew everyone in like they were on the edge of charging. The parade continued and large characters beginning to walk amongst a wall of performers. These characters were carried by about a dozen people. They were as tall as buildings and moved sporadically with the beat of the drums.

The young man and Juliana took a walk back to the hotel as she need to use the ladies' room, and while he waited outside on the front steps an old lady came up and looked into his eyes. She didn't say anything for a while, but then said she saw the pain of his past and took his hand. She said was happy he was here on this very day, celebrating, then handed him a Mexican honeysuckle and walked off. Juliana walked out at this moment and took hold of the young man from behind. The young man was puzzled by what had just happened. He told Juliana about the lady and she, too, was puzzled. They left the parade and made their way to meet Maria at the party, walking through the streets which glowed and were full of life.

The party was at an old factory turned nightclub. Maria was waiting outside for them and introduced them to her friends. As they all went in, it seemed as though all the people from the parade had come to this one party. It was hot but not a nice heat, a stuffy humid heat that was sweat inducing. The young man took off his jacket and hung it over a wooden banister in the club – never to be seen again! He was down to just a black shirt. Both the young man's and Juliana's make-up started wearing off and dripping down their faces due to the sweat. If their make-up wasn't scary before, it was now! They looked like Delilah before she was fixed up, paint peeled flakes formed. The club had lots of small stages that wrapped around the edge of the building, everybody dancing like it was their last night on earth. The young man and Juliana hadn't seen this kind of passionate dancing since Buenos Aires at Santiago's and Isabella's club, El Sonrisa. They loved it and a yearning to dance took control of them. The young man rolled up his sleeves while looking deep into Juliana's eyes. She gave a cute little smile and then they danced. The room, for them, emptied with each step, each movement, each breath they took, and these were all expressions of passion and freedom.

They partied the night away for the next hour then the young man and Juliana got separated. He had gone to get some drinks but on the way back he couldn't see her. She was with Maria, but the young man couldn't see her either. While he searched for her, a man was starting to get a little too close and hands on with Juliana. She was trying to push him away, but he was persistent and was gradually getting more aggressive because she kept turning him away. She couldn't get out as there were people all around her blocking her exits. The young man, now seeing Juliana and this man who was grabbing her, ran through the crowds, pushing people out of the way to get to her. The young man pushed him away from her and swung for him, knocking him to the ground. The young man was standing with Juliana now behind him. He stood there ready to fight for Juliana, but Juliana grabbed the young man's hand, pulled him away and they left before more trouble erupted.

Once outside, Juliana had a smirk on her face. She tugged on the young man's shirt and pulled him close. Getting on her tiptoes, she kissed him, they then walked off into the night along candlelit streets back to the hotel. Juliana still had a smirk on her face while she held onto the young man's arm. Maria had caught up with them with a few of the friends they had just met.

Maria said, "How about we have our own celebration? A private party for us in the hotel bar – it will be closed now." Once at the hotel, Maria told them all to be quiet as they would get in trouble if they got caught. Maria had a key to the bar for emergencies, and Maria was a rebel.

"Well, this is an emergency, isn't it?" she said. "We need to celebrate life. If that's not an emergency then I don't know what is!"

Once they had snuck into the bar, Maria closed and bolted the bar door, then went behind the counter and got some ice. She wrapped it up in a bar cloth and placed it on the young man's hand, which had started to bruise. The young man, Juliana, Maria and her friends spent the evening at the bar drinking tequila, dancing, and had a little sing along. The hotel bar had a rustic, distressed look: the walls were covered in old posters, the bar had an ebony countertop, two old grand chandeliers hung from the ceilings. A jukebox rested in the corner. They turned it on to play Latin music. One of Maria's friends was holding the jukebox, moving her hips and legs to the rhythm of the music, looking for a song she wanted to play next.

Maria turned out the lights; she thought she heard someone. The only light left came from the neon one behind the bar, an orange stripe that lit up the drinks, making the devil's juice look even more appealing than it already was. The neon light bounced off the bottles and lit up the room, the chandeliers reflected it across the room, with beams going off in all directions. To the sound of Latin music, the young man and Juliana started dancing. Juliana felt a few drops of water trickle down her back from the melting ice on the young man's hand.

"This is much better than that party," he said. "Me and you can dance the night away."

"I want to dance every night away with you," Juliana answered.

With their heads resting together and their lips nearly touching, the young man said, "Well, I'm a lucky man, because I want to dance every night away with you." They grinned, slowly and passionately kissed, then continued dancing.

One of Maria's friends was a singer although she was shy and didn't like singing in front of people. However, with a little encouragement from everyone and a little tequila, she got up on stage and sang. Her voice was heavenly, and set a mood of passionate tranquillity. Another friend picked up a guitar that was in the back room and started playing, the strings being lit up by the orange neon aiding the lady on stage.

After Maria's friend had sung her song, she wanted to stop but the young man walked up to the stage saying, "Oh no, you don't. We're going to do a duet!"

The lady said, "No ... wait, you can sing?"

The young man, giggling to himself, replied, "I guess we'll find out in a second." They both smiled at each other. The young man took the microphone out of the stand and started belting out a classic ballad. Maria's friend started singing with him after he smiled pointed the microphone at her. It is safe to say the young man wouldn't have a career as a singer, but the duet made everyone smile and soon Maria's friend's nerves settled down. Eventually everyone was singing. They all got behind the microphones and pretend to perform for a roaring crowd of adoring fans who begged for more. Everyone was taking it in turns to be centre stage and the others seamlessly fell in an unorganised organised backing group, all giving unique but equally memorable performances.

Exhausted from the singing, they sat at the bar to hydrate with tequila. Maria raised her glass and said, "To my dear grandmama, and to all those we've lost and hold dear." She then went on, saying, "My grandmama was the best. On one of our last conversations together she told me to keep a childlike spirit and hold it tight and never let it go. She said life was a lot more fun with a childlike spirit; she said, play games, explore with a yearning to learn, be brave and keep the enthusiasm of a rocket going to space. She said a childlike spirit kept the mind young. She truly was an amazing woman."

The young man said, "She sounded like a wise lady. The old man I told you about said the same thing to me once."

"Yes, she was," said Maria with a smile. "But she was crazy too ... well, he was a wise man as well."

They all laughed, and the young man raised his glass and said, "To crazy grandmama." The rest of the night was filled with much more tequila, much more dancing and many more good times.

The next day slowly arrived. Maria and her friends had all gone home in the early hours of the morning. The young man and Juliana spent the rest of the morning and the early afternoon in bed, paying the price for the memories they had made the night before. They had a couple more days in Mexico City which they spent with Maria and her friends but their time there had come to an end. They had to go back to Guatemala to meet William and Arabella. As they closed the door and made their way down the grand staircase, Maria was waiting for them at reception as she knew they were leaving today. They hugged and said farewell. The young man and Juliana had spoken about some of the down sides to travelling and thought one of the very few of them was saying goodbye to newfound friends. The found it was like a little break-up every place you went. Maria had got them a taxi and it was waiting outside. She followed them out to the street and waved them farewell as they drove off.

After a long journey they were back in Guatemala, met up with William and Arabella straight away and had dinner. They walked down the street of the small coastal town where they had stopped off before heading to Mexico. The street had no paths and all the buildings had either corrugated or thatched roofs. Palm trees were everywhere making a rustling sound in the wind. Most of the locals drove scooters and they could hear the revving of the engines from a mile away every so often.

They arrived at a little restaurant, and William said, "This place does amazing food. We love it here. Best restaurant for miles. Well, to be honest, it's the only restaurant for miles but the food is still good." The young man and Juliana laughed, they had dinner and to their surprise, it was good. They spent the evening on William and Arabella's yacht talking about the future. William asked them what they intended to do after they had travelled. The young man was stumped – he hadn't really thought about what he would do afterwards, and the old man didn't leave any advice for after he had travelled. Juliana didn't really know what the future held either. They were both a little lost when thinking about the future, there was too much choice and the young man had been dealing with depression and his mental health for so long that he had never really had a chance to think about what to do with his life. He was always focused on surviving the day ahead that the future didn't even come into consideration. The young man and Juliana were a pair of lost souls.

William and Arabella had got to know the young man and Juliana quite well now, they had spent countless evenings talking and they really liked them both personally and intellectually.

Arabella said to the young couple, "Once you have finished your travels, we would love for you to join the team and work at the foundation with us. That's if you want to, of course. There's no pressure, it's an option you guys now have. We do work all over the globe, so the travelling won't end." Arabella also told them not to give an answer, they were in no rush for one. The young man and Juliana, both smiling, said thank you.

William, with a smirk, then said, "You both have made an impression on us."

They spent the remainder of the evening looking at the stars, sipping on their drinks and telling stories. While they were talking, the young man thought about how much he loved stories and poetry. He thought they were a gift but, at times, a gift people could take for granted. The ability to tell a story and comprehend it is a gift in itself and the young man loved to be taken away into his imagination where the stories he was told could come alive.

After a few more days in Guatemala, they said goodbye to William and Arabella at the docks. They were staying there as they had some work to do for their foundation and liked the peacefulness this little town provided. So the young man and Juliana set sail again, this time up Mexico's west coast.

They enjoyed the journey; they surfed, they dined, and they explored together. They continued to grow closer with each passing day. And with each day they learned something new about each other, whether it was a new quirk, an old story, a new dream, or desire. The young man and Juliana had made a deal with each other back in Brazil that they would constantly learn about one another. They had realised quickly that they were in a changing world and were changing people. And quite honestly, they looked forward to learning something new about the other.

They arrived at the coastal town of Puerto Vallarta and they slowly navigated the marina, giving nods and waves of acknowledgement to all the other seafarers already docked. They arrived as the sun was setting, so decided to spend the evening in the marina and wait until dawn to go and explore the city.

In the morning, a lady in the marina told Juliana that the romantic zone/old town was a must-see in Puerto Vallarta. So, when she saw the young man, she told him. Her excitement got him excited so they went to explore the city. A small taxi ride later and they were in the old town, which immediately they fell in love with. This place had so much character and every little detail added something to the feeling you got while walking the streets. The old town was beautiful, and especially a particular street that had a cobbled road which was bowed at the edges. It had white buildings with green balconies and multi-coloured bunting hung across the street from home to home like a lifeline connecting everyone. Flowers and trees flourished everywhere, from hanging baskets on the balconies to the streets to flower beds in the shops, to palm trees that lined the cobbled street.

The young man and Juliana had lunch and then got themselves a hotel room. They loved sailing and living on Delilah but immersing yourself in the places you go is half the fun so they liked staying in hotels when they could. They felt it made the experience more authentic, plus clean sheets each night wasn't too bad either. They found a hotel in the old town and in their room they had a view which at first was hidden behind wooden shutters. When opened, the view bewitched them. They were struck by a background of oceanic blues, then a sea of red tiles, purple flowers that peered into view from the ledge by the window. In centre of this view, there was a cathedral with a steeple that had a metal crown with a cross on top. This crown shared features of a rose. From the young man and Juliana's eyes, it looked like four huge metal petals with intricate lace patterns that elegantly folded up to a symbol of hope for many. The sun shone on the cathedral steeple and through the metal petals creating silhouettes on the buildings behind.

Although the hotel room was nice, they didn't stay long. They put fresh shirts on and ventured back out into the streets of Puerto Vallarta in the hope of finding more food. On the walk the young man and Juliana came across a boxing gym. It was simply called Miguel's; on the sign there were two boxing gloves either side. The young man walked in and booked himself in for a class the next day. Boxing wasn't really Juliana's thing, so she made other plans; she was going to sit in a café and draw. They liked having some time apart. It could get quite intense being on that boat all day and night together. A little time apart was good, more than good, it was healthy. Plus, being away from each other for a small amount of time made them miss one another and they thought it was nice to have their own stories to tell when they met again. Everyone needs time alone with their thoughts and their demons.

The young man arrived at the gym, anxiously awaiting his

session. He had never boxed before or had a fight for that matter, so this would all be completely new to him and he didn't have the slightest clue what to expect. As he walked into the gym, his anxiety spiked a little. But only for a moment as his attention soon was taken by how he loved the gyms raw functionality. The gym was in an old textile factory with shutter doors leading in from the streets. At the entrance there was a desk where the young man had to sign a waiver.. Huge industrial fans blowed cool air around the gym and boxing bags lined one wall. The boxing rings were in the middle of the warehouse and that made each fighter feel like a monument to the sport. The young man was met at the entrance by an old man; his name was Miguel. He told the young man that he was having a one-to-one session as nobody else had booked onto the class.

Straight away Miguel had the young man running laps in the gym and doing a variety of movements to warm him up. Miguel wouldn't tell the young man when it was going to end, he just gave him the next movement. He was testing the young man's will power to carry on with no end in sight. Miguel did tell the young man this was just the warmup and the young man laughingly in pain said, "You're joking, right?" Miguel just sadistically smiled and said no.

The warm up ended and the young man put on gloves. Miguel put on pads and they started practising some drills.

The young man was exhausted by the end of the session. Juliana was waiting for him outside. They walked down a few streets and had lunch in a little café on the corner of a side street. Juliana had been drawing in the café while the young man was at the gym, she had been there all morning but had waited for the young man before getting food. She didn't like eating alone but her mouth had watered all morning. They ordered and watched the world go by. While they waited for the food to arrive, Juliana showed the young man her drawing; she had drawn the street to picture quality.

The next day the young man had another session at the gym with Miguel and this session was even more pain inducingly hard than the previous day's session. Miguel kept saying throughout the session "never end the fight". This kept the young man going; having Miguel shouting encouragement would keep anyone going. The young man hit the pads, one, two, three, then if the young man looked like he was going to quit, Miguel shouted, "Never end the fight!" and they would go on, the young man continuing to hit the pads, one, two, three. The further into the session they went, the more the young man realised he had more to give and when he hit another wall, he soon realised he had more to give.

They sat down on the edge of the ring for a breather and the young man told Miguel, "I liked what you said. It helped me keep going. I was so close to stopping."

Miguel said, "It's something I teach all my students. It's a tool to keep in our mental arsenal that will serve you well. 'Never end the fight' means so many things in so many situations, but simply means 'don't quit, never surrender'. We always have more to give. If you have a problem, don't stop until you find a solution; when you think you're done you have just entered the realm of unknown potential. It all comes down to our state of mind. If we believe, we can do. The mind and body are capable of unbelievable things if we have a little determination and trust in our potential."

The young man was sitting on the edge of the ring, listening and nodding. Miguel continued, saying, "There's always another way, another route. Well, most the time there is. There are a few rare occasions where there's no other way, but as a general rule, there is always something that can be done, or something else to try."

Once the breather was over, Miguel and the young man continued training, and once the session had finished, they went for a walk and Miguel told him a story about his past. He started telling a story of being in the cartel, finding Buddhism and now living the life he loves with his boxing gym.

Miguel said, "My story starts as a teenager in poverty. I joined the cartel because I was trying to provide for my family; we were really poor, and my dad had been killed when I was thirteen by the very cartel I would soon be a part of. I needed to put food on the table for my family. I had younger brothers and sisters to care for now. My mum had been flattened by life and the death of my father, so I had no choice but to become the parent and provide. So, I started out doing deliveries for the cartel when I was a young teenager. I did that for about a year. And after that job I became a debt collector. I had to collect all the money owed to the cartel in my given area. I did this for a while, then I was told I had to make a point to some locals that they had to pay their debts on time, so I had to kill a man to make the point and prove my loyalty. If I didn't do so, I would have been killed myself. I can still remember the man's face, clear as day, and I go to sleep with it each night. It was raining that afternoon. The streets become muddy and tin roofs being rained on sounded like gunfire. I dragged the man out of his home and threw him in the mud. I can still hear his pleading voice in my dreams. Please, please, I'll get you the money, please! All the neighbours were out crying. For a moment I hesitated but a higher member of the cartel was there watching my every move. I shot him and left him bleeding in the mud; a river of blood ran down the street and over my shoes. His wife and kids were keeling in the mud, crying and screaming. The second I pulled the trigger I was no longer the same man. I remember thinking as I walked away about that little boy who had lost his father to evil, and I couldn't help but think whether I had put him on the same path I was on. A few years went by and along the way I had to make a few more points, and before I even knew it, I had become an assassin for the cartel. I had slowly been stripped back and remoulded into a man I didn't recognise anymore. It was such a slow and subtle transformation that in the moment you couldn't tell. It's only when looking back I can see what happened. Each task they gave me got a little worse in its nature, more cruel, more evil, more demonic, more monstrous. And with each task it made my tolerance for evil grow. It had gradually risen without me even really knowing or objecting; I had slowly morphed into evil. I did unforgivable atrocities to so many people and communities all in service for a group who stripped me of my humanity and my youth. That's why I set up the gym. I wanted to create a sanctuary for all those kids who could be poached by the cartels, destined to die young. So many young men die in service of the cartels barely making it to twenty four. I was lucky in some sense to have survived, but before I set up the gym and found Buddhism, I envied those who had died.

"But one day I woke up and felt different. I don't know why; nothing had really changed. I was just tired both physically and mentally. I was walking down this random street in a city I was temporarily in and I found Buddhism by pure chance. I stumbled into a lady handing out leaflets advertising a Buddhism retreat. I don't know why but I took the leaflet.

CHAPTER 11

Normally I wouldn't have even acknowledged her existence but I felt an urge inside so I took it and in my hotel room later that night I spent hours staring at each page. I must have read every word a hundred times. In the morning I rang the number on the leaflet and booked myself on it. A couple of days later I was in the retreat, off the grid and away from my dark demonic world. During the retreat I had to come face to face with my demons, isolated in the depths of my psyche. I was guided through by the monks, but I was alone with my thoughts. When it comes to the mind, there's only one person who can walk through the door, and that person is you. I had to confront the aspects of myself that I had hidden deep down. I did this through reflection, self-analysis, and meditation. The solitude of the retreat was oddly comforting and the feeling of being in a group of people that were all confronting the dragon which they were going to slay and free themselves of the mental misery in which they resided, was also comforting. Only the brave get to slay the dragon, because to do that you have to have the courage to confront it and know you might get burned. A couple of days into the retreat I found that meditation soon became a backbone of my recovery and new self-discovery. On the retreat we would meditate three times a day as a group on a small pagoda on the lake. Each time I meditated I went further and further into the maze of my mind; some would lead to dead ends but with more and more practice I reached the centre of my maze and it was liberating. My journey to free my mind from the fiery pits of hell was a long and gradual process and, to be really honest, a process I'm still on. It is a never-ending process. I had to accept my past and choose to live in the present. One of the monks told me something that changed my world. While we walked through the gardens which were as zen as the buddha himself, windy paths with grey gravel, the sounds of water trickling down little streams and dropping off the edges of rocks, greenery and flowers encircling you from all directions he told me, "What we think we become, what we feel we attract, what we imagine we create." He paused a few moments to let his words sink in and continued to tell me that we control everything, we control if we are happy, if we are sad, if we are anxious, we control everything, we need to remain mindful. If we want to become happy, think happy. If we want to attract happiness, feel happiness. If we want to create happiness, imagine it.

"I would go on long walks around the gardens with one of the monks who was leading the retreat, we had made a little routine of meeting together after morning meditation for these walks. I told him about my past and the things I had done. He would listen intently and offered words of wisdom and new perspectives. It was just really nice to have someone who wanted to help you.

"I gradually peeled back the layers of my mind, memory by memory, thought by thought, trigger by trigger and with each layer I peeled back I began to feel free. I saw clarity when I looked into a pool of water in the gardens while walking with the monk because for the first time in decades I recognised the reflection. I spent weeks in the retreat and when I left, I was a changed man. As I walked out of the gates, I knew I was going to leave the cartel, how it would be one of two ways – death, or liberation. I was surprisingly allowed to leave – I had been loyal and honest for decades and for that I was allowed to go in peace. I expected to die and was ready for it; I had met my demons and bid them farewell. For the first time since I killed that man in the rain, I was free and content with my existence.

CHAPTER 11

"They let me leave on the condition that I disappear, never to be seen by them again. So, after I left, I came here to Puerto Vallarta. I got all my tattoos removed, painful procedures over many months, so I could really let go of my past and focus on being in the present and look forward to the future."

After they got back from the walk, Juliana was sitting on a brick wall waiting for the young man and when she saw him she jumped down and smiled. Miguel and hugged and the young man said, "If we never meet again, I want you to know you will forever be in my heart and mind." Miguel then patted the young man on the shoulder and said, "And you mine." They then said their final goodbyes.

With that final goodbye it was also time for the young man and Juliana to say goodbye to Puerto Vallarta. They set off to sail up the Mexican coast to a secluded isolated beach; they had rented an old stone house there for the week. Juliana was going to paint, and the young man was going to write, and together they were going to surf. The day after they arrived, they got a delivery from a young boy on a bicycle – just some food and supplies they needed. The lady they were renting the house from had offered to provide food and supplies at a small additional cost.

The isolation provide clarity in Juliana's painting and the young man's writing. Being away from the world is good for the mind and soul; you can recalibrate and focus on your innermost thoughts.

Juliana sat on the little stone porch that overlooked the Pacific Ocean and the Mexican countryside while she painted. She found that very spot creative heaven. The young man found wandering their new surroundings helpful for his writing. Every day while they were at the little stone house, he sat in the kitchen looking through the big double doors which overlooked the sea. The young man found it soothing and the doors acted as a frame for the beautiful artwork and one of his many loves – the sea.

A long time ago now the old man had told him to keep a diary, but now the young man wrote more than diaries. He wrote poems, short stories and even begun a novel, well, ideas, at the moment they were scribbles in his diary. While on his daily wander, feet in the sand, the breeze blowing his shirt back like a cape, he sat down facing the ocean and let his mind rattle around ideas and gather thoughts. He wrote:

"The beauty of life is living a poetic life, a poetic life is an emotional life, an emotional life is a life of experiences, a life of experiences is a life of doing, and doing is all we can do. So by being and doing we are all poets."

While the young man wrote on the beach, Juliana was painting some of her best work on that little porch, in that little house, on that little stretch of Mexican isolation. Every day the young man would bring her coffee in the morning and would whisper these words into her ear.

"Now, tomorrow, forever, my love."

He then kissed her on the neck and walked back into the kitchen. He sat at the table watching her paint while drinking his morning coffee before going about his day. The young man brought the vinyl player from the boat into the house and set it up in one of the rooms that overlooked the sea. He and Juliana were in there that late afternoon for hours, lying on the floor, taking in the music, just vibing to the melodies.

In the evening ,while Juliana was cooking, the young man sat on the kitchen table, crossed legged, reading another one of the old man's letters. He had been searching through the

CHAPTER 11

old battered box for hours and had finally found what he was looking for – the letters of the time he first met Ruby. The young man began reading the letters aloud, and yet again the old man's words transported them back in time. This letter took them to 1969 in the Sea of Marmara. The old man was on route to Istanbul, Turkey.

The old man was sailing into Istanbul, still under the cover of the night but the sun was beginning to rise as he got closer to the city. While sailing in, the old man thought how cool it was that he had Europe on his left and Asia on his right. The city was beautiful from where the old man was, the blue mosque and the Hagia Sophia were in view, which took the breath away from the old man, as it must have for all other sailors that have had the pleasure of sailing into Istanbul.

The old man moored up in a marina overlooking the western side of the city – only a bridge connected the two. Once he secured the boat and was on land, he headed straight for wherever he could smell food. He found a street food vendor selling what could only be described as heaven. He had Balık Ekmek, a grilled fish sandwich of sorts. He sat on a wall overlooking the city with his sandwich and a cup of Turkish tea. After a couple of bites he put down both the tea and sandwich, picked up his camera and took pictures. He loved capturing moments of truth, an honest moment, nothing pre-planned, just acts of truthful spontaneity. The old man up to this point had made a living doing odd jobs for people where ever he went, but he wanted to be a photographer and hopefully make a bit of money from it. Not enough to support himself – he liked to think of himself as a struggling artist who was a part of an elite club of people willing to starve for their art and spend a lifetime perfecting it, never accepting the quality of yesterday. After he took a few pictures, he resumed eating this heavenly sandwich and drinking his tea.

When he had finished, he jumped up and went to explore the streets of Istanbul's Asian side, before crossing the bridge over to the city's European side, where he explored the Grand Bazaar. As he walked through the market he was immediate struck by the echoing sounds of all the haggling and chatter. The sounds were carried through the narrow walkways. The old man took a slow walk through the market, looking at all of what was being sold. The market had everything from, lamps, rugs, bags, plates, and everything else the mind could imagine. The old man was approached by nearly every vendor, persuading him that their goods were the best and that only they could give him the best price. The old man would politely say that he would have a look round first. It would take two to three polite no's before they moved onto the next person, offering them the best price.

The markets seemed to go on forever, and when he was at one stall the old man was taken away. He saw beauty, love, passion, life, and lust all in a single moment. He saw a woman. He walked with speed thought the small walkways of the Grand Bazaar, trying to catch up to this lady who was now walking away. He was jumping in and out of people, and at times barging people, although he would turn around and quickly say sorry. She had vanished. The old man stopped and looked around, but he couldn't see her or where she could have gone. He dropped back down from where he was standing and left the Grand Bazaar. He went to a little café to drown his sorrows with the best tea he had ever had. He spent much of the afternoon in the café. No need to rush when you travel, he thought. He just sat and watched people go about their day, but mostly he thought about that woman and he vividly recreated her in his mind. The restaurant owner had seen the old man stay there most of the afternoon and came up to him. They talked, and he gave the old man a tea on the house.

The restaurant owner asked him, "Would you like a better view?"

The old man said, yes, so he was taken to the roof where the old man had a view of the city like no other. As the restaurant owner opened the door to the roof, the birds scattered across the sky in unison all following the leader, swarming inand flying off into the distance in search of a new resting place.

The restaurant owner said, "This is my little slice of heaven; the city seems so peaceful from up here."

The old man replied, "I think you're right; this may just be heaven."

The restaurant owner left him up there and the old man sat on the edge, feet dangled over, taking pictures of things that sparked his interest. He watched birds fly and people walk.

After the old man had finished, he walked back to his boat under the setting sun and he took a moment on the bridge looking left and right thinking how cool it was that this was the only city in the world to be in two continents. Once he had taken in this moment, the old man walked into the marina waving to all the other sailors. Once aboard he sat on the deck of Delilah with a cold beer and watched the water shape shift and glimmer in the sun. The old man had the perfect view to see the sun set. He sat at the front of the boat on his three-legged chair.

The next day the old man went to visit the Hagia Sophia. This building was born from chaos. Riots filled an ancient empire and the Hagia Sophia was built as a symbol of the greatness of the emperor and Christianity. It was rebuilt on the site of the old Hagia Sophia which had been burned down during the riots. The old man chose to go on a walk round tour with a guide who told the group that the Hagia Sophia was built a little over fourteen hundred years ago, and that it was originally built as a cathedral but later, when the Ottoman Empire took control, it was converted into a mosque, and now for the past 35 years it has been a museum. The guided tour started in the botanic gardens which were stunning and had windy paths that led to the entrance. Before they went inside, the guide took the opportunity to tell them the history behind the building. The old man took the moment to capture a truthful moment; his truthful moment was that of looking at the Hagia Sophia. He looked and was taken away by its beauty.

The old man and his tour group walked inside and the building was an architectural marvel. The domed roof captivated your attention instantly. The dark charcoal coloured walls were bold and drew your attention to the symbols on the walls. In the old man's eyes, they looked like giant shields. These shields had golden Arabic words on them. There was a mustard yellow ceiling with ancient artwork. The building was a fusion between Christianity and Islam with over a thousand years of history seeped into its walls.

The old man looked up. He stood still and spun round slowly, looking at each and every detail. The tiles were stunning mosaics, masterpieces that had been preserved through time. Some of the tiles were worn but the old man liked it as it added character and made you feel the age of the building. What the old man loved the most was that all the curves of the building flowed. Each dome or arch seemed to gracefully lead to the next. The building was both soft and harsh; the ceiling was soft, but the walls were harsh. Their stonework, although beautiful, was sharp and dark. Little windows that wrapped around the main dome let light in and it mixed with the mustard colour on the ceiling, giving the feeling of a flame in a candle.

The old man wandered the streets of Istanbul after the tour had finished. He wanted to find some food, but what he found was a lot better. He found the woman he had seen in the Grand Bazaar. His heart was racing, his legs had gone to jelly and his mind was running wild. The old man went up to her and introduced himself. She was waiting in line for some street food.

"Hi, I'm Richard," he said.

She was a little startled then said, "Hi, I'm Ruby."

The old man told her the story of the Grand Bazaar and how he had thought he would never see her again. Ruby was flattered and smiled.

"Well, Richard, would you like to have lunch with me?" she asked.

His heart began to settle — he hadn't been rejected. The old man said, "Yes, I would love to."

They walked and talked and made their way to the Blue Mosque. The old man had been going to go there, and Ruby hadn't seen inside yet.

The old man and Ruby spent the remainder of the day together. He asked her if she would like to meet again the next day. Ruby said she had plans with some people she had met in her hostel, but said she was free for dinner.

"Dinner it is then," the old man said.

The next day soon arrived and dinner went more than well. Ruby had planned to go to Greece in the coming days and the old man said he was going to go too. In reality, he didn't he just didn't want their time together to end so he offered to take her to Greece on his boat. She said yes and a couple of days later they were sailing away. By the time they got to Greece they had both fallen in love and that's where the adventure started for them both. They explored Greece then the rest of the world together.

By the time the young man had read the old man's letters and diary entries, Juliana placed dinner on the table and they sat with the Mexican moon in view through the window. They ate and chatted about the old man's Turkish adventure.

They had been at this stone haven for a few days now and had enjoyed the break from the intensity of travelling constantly. Sometimes a break is needed to ease the mind. They had been mentally and visually stimulated for months on end, so a week to unwind with just the two of them was heavenly. While the young man showered, he asked Juliana to have a look at his writing. She flicked through the pages and, as they ran across her thumb, she stopped the book at a random page that felt right. She read:

"Be like a flower, blossom, blossom, blossom. You may be picked for a moment of your beauty, or you may be preserved and admired, or you may be left in the dirt. But blossom, blossom, blossom. Be like a flower.".

She sat down at the table where the young man sat and flicked through his book. The pages were all crinkled and had lots of aggressive crossings out and little adjustments covered the page. The pages didn't look like much but the words on them were songs of the soul.

Their Mexican adventure would be over soon and they made the most of the paradise they had found themselves in. On their last night, the young man and Juliana had their own private party on the beach. They swam in the sea, danced to crappy

CHAPTER 11

music around a little fire, made up stories as they looked into the stars, drank wine and they then made their way back to the house and started painting with drunken inspiration. The sea air woke them up on the stone house's roof, cuddled up together. They made their way to the porch where they took in the view before they sailed off into the distance.

Chapter 12

The young man and Juliana had left Mexico and were now beginning to leave the relative safety of the coastal waters they had enjoyed for some time now. Although the young man had sailed across the Atlantic, but they had gone many months now with the safety of seeing land and he was a little nervous to be crossing the largest ocean in the world. The first day of sailing was blissful; the ocean was calm, and the sun shone brightly. Juliana was looking through a travel magazine she had bought about Hawaii, their next destination, and was talking about all the things they were going to do there. The one thing the young man really wanted to do was the 'Stairway to Heaven'.

"This is cool!" she said. "Did you know the Hawaiian Islands are a chain of one hundred and thirty-seven islands?"

"No, I didn't know that." He replied. The young man could listen to Juliana all day; the sound of her voice was soothing and went nicely with the sounds of the ocean.

As they sailed across the Pacific en route to Hawaii, the seas were calm and everything was still, not even a ripple in the water. Then came an alert on the boat's radio and navigation system, warning them that a storm was inbound. The young man had a bad feeling about this, just a gut feeling; his heart

CHAPTER 12

began to beat a little faster. But he listened to the information that was given to him on his navigation system and told himself he knew they could sail through it. It would be rough but they could sail through. Juliana began to get anxious and her breathing got heavier with each breath; she had never been in these kind of conditions before. He was worried how she would cope, and a little part of himself worried how he was going to cope, but he was confident they could get through it. He told himself this in his head over and over again; he really wanted to believe the words he was saying, so that when the time came, he was confident and could focus on the sailing. The young man told Juliana that it might be rough but they could make it. It was only classed as a category one, and by this point they were closer to Hawaii than any other big land mass, so they sailed on.

As they sailed on, little by little the sea got rougher and rougher, the clouds got darker and rain that started as a light mist soon became a heavy downpour, beating down on them. The boat, with each second passing, got pushed around more and more aggressively. The young man's grip of the wheel, standing at the helm, began slowly loosening with each wave that came crashing over the side, and the water splashed over him running down his hands. The boat now seemed to be moving in all directions. The young man had lost all control and being on that boat felt like going ten rounds with a heavyweight boxer while trying to drive a car blindfolded. It was madness. The volume of water coming onto the boat was overwhelming, coming over one side and washing over until it reunited with the ocean on the other side. The swells were growing bigger, becoming colossal in nature, a behemoth nightmare. The size of the waves made fear ravage through the mind and body of the young man and Juliana. They were soaked through to the bone and their mouths were dry from the salty water.

Water began pouring into the boat; the cabin was ingulfed in water. The young man jokingly said, "At least we don't have to pay for the onboard swimming pool anymore."

Juliana laughed and cried. "That's not funny," she said. A little humour in the presence of impending doom lightened the mood only ever so slightly and those few seconds of wicked laughter lifted their spirits. The sound of plates crashing into the walls echoed from the cabin. All the possessions the young man and Juliana owned were being tossed around, adding to the chaos surrounding them.

A colossal monster of a wave began to form. They could see it in the distance, growing with vengeance, taunting them as it ever so quickly came for them. It wasn't a matter of if it was going to get them, it was a matter of when; a ticking time bomb of inevitable doom. He started preparing himself for them to abandon ship. Delilah was giving a noble effort but she wouldn't survive the storm. She was fighting the ocean and if she could speak, she would have screamed, JUMP, JUMP, I CAN'T HOLD ON MUCH LONGER!

The young man looked at Juliana. "Hey, I don't want to scare you but we might have to abandon ship, I'm going to need you to get some rope and tie us together."

"What do you mean? Juliana asked. "You want us to jump off the boat?"

"I mean, we might have to jump off the boat," he said. "You need to trust me; we're going to be OK. Now, I need you to tie us together so we don't get separated."

"Yy ... yes," she mumbled, frantically looking for some rope. She stumbled over to a chest, opened it and got out the spare rope. She tied them together and then held onto the side railing, gripping it so tightly, utter panic on her face. The young man was panicking inside, but he knew he had to take control of the situation; panic would get them killed. He had to remain as calm as possible for Juliana and for himself. His confidence calmed her and reassured her a little, but panic still filled the air.

The sea broke through the glass windows at the front of the boat and water began to flood the cabin; water that had been ankle height now was hip height. Juliana quickly waded through the water, moving everything that was floating on the surface out of the way. She grabbed some pictures from the cabin and shoved them in her jacket pocket before also sending out one last mayday message over the radio, hoping someone would come to their rescue. The boat started violently swaying as it was bombarded by the ocean.

"Juliana, you OK?" the young man shouted. He didn't get a response so he shouted again, "Juliana, you OK?"

Juliana couldn't speak. She was holding onto anything not moving, trying her best not to be thrown about the cabin. The water was still rising and then suddenly the boat hit a swell, making a huge gush of water enter the cabin through the broken windows, knocking Juliana over.

"Juliana!" screamed the young man before the water came for him. He was holding on to the wheel for dear life. In the cabin, Juliana was trying to get to her feet, but every time she got up she would slip or another wave would hit and knock her back under the water. She somehow managed to get up and waded through the water once again, stumbling out of the cabin onto the deck and entered an arena of chaos. Waves looked like mountains and they roared – Juliana preferred the cabin; the walls provided a sense of safety and hid the fear that was consuming her. A colossal wave was imminent, the sea was slowing swallowing them and Delilah was really struggling now. Soon there would be only one choice and that would be to risk it, jump into the unpredictable carnage of the sea and be at her mercy.

Wave after wave crashed into them. Delilah dived straight through one wave and the boat was fully submerged, all but the mast and sails. The young man lost grip of the wheel and was taken off his feet, sliding and smashing into the railing. He clenched onto it; if he'd held it any harder, the railing would have begun to bend. The clouds sang harmonies of horror, growling with violent undertones. The young man thought this must be the gateway to hell.

They began to slowly climb a wave that quickly became vertical; it would be pure luck to reach the peak before it made the boat flip over and capsize. They kept climbing, always seeming just too far away to make it, as if the wave was teasing them. They reached the peak and for a second, and only a second, all seemed calm. The boat was no longer violently rocking and moving at missile-like speed. A second of calm later, they were thrown back into the circus and the main act was soon on. Delilah began a rapid decent, skimming the water. The young man and Juliana's stomachs were left at the top of the wave which ended with a nosedive, digging up a massive amount of water.

The young man gave Juliana a look and she knew they were going to have to abandon the boat. She began frantically panting at the fear of being in the open water and the thought of being at the mercy of the sea. This was too much for her to handle. She began checking her life jacket and the rope attached to her and the young man with shaking hands. The young man tried to calm her and comfort her. She closed her eyes for a second and took a deep breath in preparation for the task ahead.

The young man took Juliana's hand, looked into her eyes and shouted, with a smiled, "WILL YOU MARRY ME?"

Juliana shouted, "WHAT?"

"WILL YOU MARRY ME"

In the middle of all the chaos, she smiled for the first time since the seas had got rough.

"YES!" she screamed back.

"WHAT?" the young man shouted.

"YES!"

The young man smiled and they both shone, lighting up the darkness that surrounded them. But very quickly the young man's attention went back to sailing a struggling Delilah. Before they could jump overboard a rogue wave hit them from the side. The force of the wave took them off their feet, knocking them both into the dark icy waters. The waves crashed on them one after the other, dragging them down under the water.

The young man opened his eyes and it was calm, above him as he floated in weightlessness were what looked like clouds, but in fact they were waves crashing onto one another. He wanted to stay underwater – it was a lot calmer than the war which was taking place above. He then saw the clouds differently. They were no longer calm but looked like they were in combat, explosion after explosion, as the water above collided.

He then began to feel a pressure build up in his chest, as if the sea were squeezing the life out of him; his body was now panicking, needing air. As he desperately tried to swim to the surface, he could no longer hold his breath. He breathed out, with all the oxygen escaping to the surface where he craved to be. Now his chest felt like it had been hit by a truck and before his vision went black and he started to sink to the dark depths, with seconds of life left, he reached the surface, gasping for air. It was thick and joyful – a small victory. There was a brief moment to take in some oxygen before the relentless bombardment from the waves resumed and the young man began to wrestle with chaos again.

"JU ... JU ... JULIANA! JULIANA!" he immediately called out.

In the distance he could see his boat being swallowed up by the sea, the mast of the boat seemed to be holding on for dear life as the sea rapidly began to pull her to the dark depths of the ocean. One large swell later and the boat was nowhere to be seen, swallowed by the ocean.

The waves seemed even bigger now that he was floating among them, and the iciness of the water made speaking hard. The young man, now using every ounce of energy he had, tried to swim to Juliana. Using the rope she had tied round them, he swam, hoping and praying she was at the end of it. He couldn't bear the thought of her not being there. He swam as fast as he could and wrapped the rope over his shoulder and across his chest in case the ocean tried keeping them apart. And there she was, fighting to stay above the water. In her panic, she hadn't pulled the chord releasing the life jacket.

The young man grabbed hold of her. Juliana's face lit up with joy and happiness. She'd thought she was alone and was shaking in panic and fear. He was her small victory. He pulled the chords on both his and her life jackets and they held each other tightly.

In the chaotic anarchy of which the sea had become, nothing made sense, no rules applied, only hope remained; hope that

CHAPTER 12

they would survive, hope that it would end soon, hope that they would be found and rescued from this nightmare. The young man and Juliana looked at each other. For a second, they were happy that they were in each other's arms and looking into each other eyes. Nothing else mattered apart from what felt like their last chance to look at each other. Oblivious to the ravaging storm, they both whispered, "I love you" in the ears of one another. As the rain came down Biblically, all they could do was pray. Neither one of them was particularly religious but in times of desperation people tend to find a god, someone or thing who can save us and provide hope. Whether or not they believed in God or something divine, it didn't matter, the prayers they said calmed their minds and made them feel safer; to think that there was something bigger and fiercer than these swells and the ocean was comforting. They prayed over and over again.

Then, in the darkness of the night, they had a sixth sense that something was coming for them – a wave of great magnitude, on a scale incomparable and unconceivable. Their eyes dilated and their hearts sank to the ocean floor. They knew this was the wave, the destroyer of the hope which they held dearly. The wave pushed them under. They both fought to hold their breath, and when under the waves they both caught a glimpse of each other's fear and fought to get back to the surface. Once they got back there, they re-entered the anarchy. The swells seemed to be getting bigger and no relief was in sight for the young man and Juliana; they were just being thrown around by the waves.

The storm raged on throughout the night. They held each other, not knowing whether they would see daylight. Time flashed before their eyes. Their life jackets had a small light on that flashed in a slow and steady rhythm; the light flashed and reflected in the eyes of each other. This was the only light they saw for what now was blended time. The light flashed continuously throughout the night, reminding them it wasn't over, far from over.

Chapter 13

The seas were calm now; the storm was but a piece of history. And in the midst of this calmness lay two bodies in the vast expanse of the Pacific Ocean. Nothing but blue, blue sky, and blue ocean. Time was now all but a concept; they had no sense of how long they had been adrift in the ocean. It could have been weeks for all they knew, but in actual fact, had been two days. Now having no concept of time, the young man and Juliana struggled to keep their eyes open and kept drifting in and out of consciousness, after having battled the storm for hours. The mind found it hard to focus, their lips were cracked and their mouths were dry, the sea water started to look appealing. They began to think, "I'll just drink a little, just enough to make the dryness go away." They just wanted the relief of water, but every time one of them had the idea of drinking the salty water or would go to take a drink, the other one would stop them.

As they lay there, floating, the young man looked at Juliana and smiled. He looked down and tore the string off the whistle that was attached to his life jacket. Juliana had come to, and asked what he was doing. He looked into her eyes and took her hand.

He tied the string around her finger and said, "You can't have a proposal without a ring."

Juliana smiled, beaming with joy, tears rolling down her face. She put her hands on the sides of the young man's face and said, "You never fail to surprise me and I love you so much! ... could you do something for me?"

The young man said, "I love you too and I'll try my best to."

Juliana, holding back a girlish smile, asked the young man to ask her again. The young man took a few moments and he looked at her. He looked into her eyes deeply and then said, "I can't imagine my life without you. Ever since we met, the sun seems to shine brighter, and well, everything seems brighter, and I'm going to spend the rest of my life showing you how much I love you. I want to rise by the sun and dance by the moon with you for the rest of my life ... so, Juliana, will you marry me?"

"Yes," she said and she couldn't hold back the girlish smile any longer. She was radiating joy.

Juliana looking at the sea-soaked string now tied around her finger, using her thumb to spin it around. She couldn't believe being proposed to in a storm.

"Well, some good news is that we now have an amazing proposal story to tell people," she said.

They both started laughing.

"People will think we planned it!" he said.

Still laughing, Juliana said, "Why would anyone plan to go into a hurricane?"

The was laughter came from the relief and surprise at surviving the storm. Also, they laughed at being stranded in the middle of the ocean with little hope of rescue. They kept imagining and seeing boats coming to their aid, but it was their minds playing tricks on them. They had been adrift and seeing things for some time now but every time they realised it wasn't real, it didn't affect their hope. Although it was a little hope, there was still hope.

In the distance they saw what looked like a ship. They assumed it was their minds running wild and playing tricks on them again – their vision was impaired by the sun and they were both a little delirious. Juliana put her hand on her forehead, trying to block the sun.

"It's a boat!" she said. "It's a boat!"

The young man, now putting his hand on his forehead to block the sun, was trying to see for himself. A smile grew – it was a boat. But their excitement soon vanished as it was too far away and wouldn't be able to see them. Their minds hadn't played a trick on them this time; luck just wasn't on their side.

They rested their heads together in solitude. In the distance, they heard the ship's horn going off.

Juliana said, "Have they seen us? Do you think they could have heard our mayday call?"

The ship's horn went off again and they flashed a light at the young man and Juliana, letting them know they had been seen. Soon the ship got bigger; it was coming for them. It must have seen the reflection on the life jackets. Pure chance, or maybe luck was on their side. The young man and Juliana didn't care how it had happened, all that mattered was that they were coming.

As the ship got closer it sounded its horn again. With each blast of the horn their smiles grew larger and more full of life. The young man looked at Juliana and they both smiled and cried in pure relief that they were going to be OK. They floated there, watching the ship get closer until the crew got them aboard and, once inside, got them coffee and blankets. They sat next to each other in the mess hall after drying off, and didn't say anything, Juliana leaning on the young man's shoulder. This was the best cup of coffee in the world, nothing could be better than that cup of coffee. They both held it for its warmth, with their lips resting on the rims of their cups.

One of the crew came over to check on them and before she left, she said, "We watched the storm on our navigation systems. We were lucky to miss it, really. God only knows how you both survived."

Juliana looked at the young man with a cute smirk and said, "Because you have the blood of Poseidon in your veins."

The young man quietly laughed and thought of the old man. "I just think it wasn't our time; we have a lot more to do in this world and death would be a waste it."

Juliana rested her head back on the young man's shoulder and they drank their coffee, closing their eyes to be with it as it slowly brought them to the land of the living ...

A little later on, one of the crew showed them to a cabin where they could sleep and have some privacy. The second Juliana's head hit the pillow, she was asleep. The young man lay there next to her body, exhausted, but his mind was wide awake, racing over the past few days. He asked himself questions like, what if I'd turned back? What if I'd had done something different? But then he stopped himself and breathed in for four seconds and out for five. He told himself he shouldn't look back because no matter what he found, there he was, where he was, and that wasn't going to change. So, he lay there taking a moment, allowing himself to feel all the emotions he had supressed and pushed to the back of his mind during the storm. The emotions started to overwhelmed him a little but he took a deep breath and stared at the ceiling, focusing his mind. Once

CHAPTER 13

he did this, his eyes began to close. He fought to keep them open but he lost that battle and within a matter of seconds, he drifted off.

When they woke up, they had fresh clothes folded neatly on the desk for them. After changing, they walked to the mess hall and the cooks made them some breakfast.

The ship's captain came over and said, "Morning, I heard your story from one of the crew. You guys are so lucky to be alive ... I also heard you two got engaged in the middle of the hurricane and I wondered if you would like to get married? You proposed marriage in a hurricane; it seems only right to get married at sea."

The young man jumped in and said, "Don't we need to do it somewhere official?"

"On a British ship the captain can perform marriage ceremonies," the captain told them. "It would be an honour and a privilege for me to do this for you!"

The young man looked at Juliana and before he could get a word out, she looked at the young man and then the captain and said, "yes". The captain looked at the young man, making sure he was up for it as well.

The young man smiled and said to the captain, "You heard the lady!"

The captain smiled, gave them a nod, then walked off to begin arranging the ceremony. Juliana looked at the young man, pausing for a few moments just to get a look, and then kissed him. She couldn't stop smiling. She sipped the last little bit of her coffee, although she no longer needed the caffeine as the butterflies and excitement of marrying the young man gave her a shot of energy.

The crew had set up the balcony next to the bridge for the

ceremony. They lined it with life rings and used rolled up tablecloths to mark out the altar. One of the crew even went to the kitchen to get some thyme to make a bouquet for Juliana; thyme was the only thing on the ship that resembled flowers. It was rather industrially put together as they used a cable tie! Another member of the crew saw the cable tie on the bouquet and shook their head. They got a shoe string and tied a bow around the thyme. "Now that's a bouquet!" One of the ship's crew had a dress for Juliana and another had a shirt for the young man. The sun was out ,shining brightly for what was going to be happiest day of their lives. Some of the crew had come out to watch, all wearing their best clothes, which were mostly Hawaiian shirts and flower necklaces; they were much better than their dirty work clothes.

So, on that sunny afternoon, the young man and Juliana declared their love for each other on the balcony of the cargo ship in front of their rescuers.

During the ceremony, the young man and Juliana never broke eye contact, not once. The crew stood on the balcony behind the young couple; smiles and a few tears were displayed but the tears were not from who you would expect. An engineer, who was a mountain of a man, was the first one to break. He stood towards the back of the balcony and sobbed like a baby. Then, one by one, they broke; each crew member was wiping away tears from their cheeks. They didn't prepare vows – they spoke from the heart and opened their souls, spilling enough love and passion to fill an ocean. The crew's hearts melted when the young man took Juliana's hands and said, ,

"You ... I have loved you since the first day we met, and I am going to love you for as long as the sun still rises and the moon still glows. My dear, my heart, mind, soul and body are yours. I am going to love you for eons and if there is another life after this one and another one after that, then I will search for you and find you ... and love you all over again, because you are mine and I am yours. You are the reason I can't sleep at night; I stay awake because sleep seems a waste of time when I could be looking at or thinking of you. You were an unexpected delight that came into my life and you have made me question everything I knew about life, emotions and mostly love. My soul feels like it has lived a thousand lives and in those thousand lives it has been endlessly searching, endlessly searching for you. When it found you, it caught alight with passion and love and my soul felt at home with yours. I get lost in your eyes and your words. Every day I find a new reason why I love you. You make me a better man and I'm going to spend the rest of my life showing you how much I love and care for you. Now, let me tell you a little secret; there's not a moment in the day when I'm not thinking about you and especially about kissing you. You are my greatest poem and my love for you is my greatest story. I am the luckiest man to be standing here in front of you, and the thought of calling you my wife fills my heart with joy."

Juliana's eyes had tears building up. She smiled and then said her vows. She declared her love for the young man in front of everyone and tried holding back her tears while speaking. They then said, I do, and kissed, and as they kissed, one of the crew gave a signal they sounded the ship's horn. It was the crew's way of celebrating and toasting the young man and Juliana into marriage. They stood holding each other, looking at all the smiling faces of the crew, then looked at each other again and the young man wrapped his hand behind Juliana's neck and kissed her. They walked down the balcony with the crew linking arms above them, making a wave as they walked through. The captain was clapping and smiling as he watched the young couple take the first steps of their next chapter together. All the crew hugged the young man and Juliana but once the ceremony was over, most of the crew had to go back to work, so the young man and Juliana danced in the mess hall, each with one earphone in. They pressed shuffle play on the music; whatever song played would be their song from now on. The chefs in the kitchen watched while they prepared the evening's meal, smiling through the serving hatch.

Juliana said to the young man, "We couldn't have planned this day better if we'd wanted to."

The young man smiled and said, "No, we couldn't have, my love. Well, maybe not the storm, I think I could live without the storm."

They danced to one song and they played that one song on repeat over and over again, and each time it played they fell deeper and deeper into each other. Their souls, hearts and bodies weaved together and neither one stopped smiling. These smiles would be on their faces for a long time to come. While smiling, they looked into each other's eyes, heads resting together.

Later that day, the young man took a walk up to the bridge to go outside. He stood leaning on the balcony railing, on the spot where he had married Juliana overlooking the vast expanse of the Pacific Ocean. For a moment he wondered if the old man's three-legged chair had survived the storm. If it had, he liked to think it was washed ashore on some beach somewhere and had been found by a passer-by who, when they looked at it, would feel the thousands of stories it held and that they would give it some more stories to store. He also had a vision of one day coming across the chair in some far away land, and with a little luck, be reunited with it.

After his daydream, the young man wrote one more diary entry into the now crinkled and salt-soaked book (which he had manged to save during the storm). He flicked through the pages until he found a blank one. The young man stood on the balcony, hugged by his roll neck jumper which the captain had given to him, pencil at the ready with the wind gently blowing the hair from his face. The young man wrote:

"I want to rise by the sun, and dance by the moon.

For my journey is short,

As long as a piece of string.

I want to be as the wind drifting in the sky,

Touching souls wherever I go.

I want to be rain and I want to rain on a place where I can play all day.

I want to be as free as a bird,

Following the compass of my heart.

I want to play air guitar in the street,

And eat ice cream in the rain.

I want to love,

but love only one.

I want to be a rogue, a rebel, a pioneer.

But most of all I want to be free and me."

The young man closed the book and held it, rubbing his thumbs over the cover. Juliana came out and hugged him from behind. He put his arm around her and they smiled at each other.

The young man said, "I love you ... what should we do now?" Juliana then said,

"We can do anything we want; there's a whole world out there for us to see. As long as we are together. But all I know right now is I want you to hold me," Juliana answered.

They both held each other tight and watched the sun set. Just before it dropped below the horizon, the young man whispered to himself and the old man, "I'm going to rise by the sun and dance by the moon."

Afterword

Thank you for reading! If you enjoyed the book please leave a review, tell your friends, spread the word and Rise by the Sun Dance by the Moon.

Keep a look out for the next book!